ROCK CHICK BONUS TRACKS

ROCK CHICK SERIES

KRISTEN ASHLEY

ROCK CHICK
PRESS

Rock Chick

BONUS TRACKS

A ROMANCE NOVEL BY
NEW YORK TIMES BESTSELLING AUTHOR

KRISTEN ASHLEY

Cover Image: Pixel Mischief Design

TRACK 1
ROCK CHICK

HIS LIST

Lee

Lee was in the extra bedroom in his condo sorting through the stuff, most of which would be trashed, when he heard the front door open.

He stilled, listening.

That was he stilled all but his hand. Automatically, it crept to his weapon that was sitting on the beat-up metal desk beside him.

Then he heard strange scraping sounds coming from the door handle, like someone was attempting, poorly, to pick the lock.

"Jesus," he muttered, stood, and leaving the gun where it was, he walked to the door.

He pulled it open and watched Indy's body jolt so strongly, she lost balance in the crouch she was holding on the balls of her flip-flopped feet and fell to her ass in the hall.

She looked up at him.

"It was open," he informed her.

"Oh," she replied.

"So no need to pick the lock," he shared unnecessarily as she started to push up to standing.

"Yeah, I got that," she returned irritably, brushing off her ass with one hand, even though the hall was carpeted, and Judy kept it obsessively vacuumed.

He didn't watch her brush her ass. He watched as a flush formed on her beautiful cheeks. Color, Lee knew, that didn't come from embarrassment, because as far as he could tell, his woman didn't get embarrassed. And fuck knew, he'd witnessed her giving herself plenty of opportunity to feel embarrassment.

No, she was annoyed.

She was also curious.

In many instances, he could read her mind—this was how long he'd known her, and how much attention he'd paid to her—but this time she made it easy.

She tried to peer beyond him.

She'd always been nosy, including being nosy about a room in his place that he kept locked.

Her place was now his place, which prompted him sorting that room. He should have done it before, but now he had renters moving in, so he had to see to it.

Considering his woman's most recent antics, he wasn't going to make it easy for her to get what she wanted.

He stood solid in the doorframe and kept the information flowing.

"You do remember three weeks ago? You know, that time when you were kidnapped...*again*...and nearly taken against your will to Costa Rica?"

Her amazing blue eyes darted to him, and Christ.

Give him a year, even five, to think on it, and he couldn't tell you precisely what did it for him with her.

This was because there was so much of her that did it for him.

Those eyes, for starters. That blue—rich and so fucking deep, not dark, not light, an azure so pure, he could swim in it.

Her ample ass and tits were two others.

The fact she was who she was, did what she did, let it all hang out and didn't get embarrassed about any of it was high on the list too.

"That's hard to forget," she retorted, a hint of snap in her tone.

"And you thought it was a good idea to creep around my condo?"

"I wasn't creeping. I have a key."

"You have absolutely no reason to be here. You were creeping."

She made the wise decision not to reply to that.

"And I have a gun," he went on.

She rolled her eyes.

Fair play, he'd never shoot anyone he didn't intend to shoot, and they both knew it.

"You're a trouble magnet," he muttered.

She rolled her eyes again.

Another fair play, Indy being that wasn't news.

He let his gaze drop to her hand, the one she didn't use to brush off her ass.

He returned it to her face. "Is that my lock picking kit?"

"Um..." She didn't exactly answer.

"You stole my lock picking kit?"

"I didn't steal it." Definitely a snap in that. "I found it."

"You found it," he repeated wryly.

"I found it."

She was such a shit liar.

"I hid it in one of my boots so you wouldn't do something like, oh, I don't know..." He gestured to the floor between them and finished, "*This.*"

She scrunched up her nose and kept her mouth shut.

He knew why.

She was dying to see what was in the room behind him and getting into an argument with him might mean she wouldn't get what she wanted.

"You know, if you wanted to know what was in this room, there's ways to find out that don't involve breaking and entering," he pointed out.

"Naked gratitude?" she asked snottily.

He grinned. "Well, yeah. That's always an option."

Her stare turned to a glare.

He went on, "But also, you could just ask."

She put a hand on her hip, hitched said hip—always a warning coming from any female, a code red warning coming from Indy—and asked, fake-sweetly, "Can I see what's in there?"

"Sure," he replied easily.

She blinked in surprise, and Lee moved out of her way.

She walked in and gazed around.

Lee watched her.

Her gorgeous, expressive face was filled with wonder.

Another of those things that did it for him. The fact she was gorgeous, but more, how free she was with her expressions. She gave her trust like the precious gift it was, and she gave it openly. Then it was up to you what you did with it.

She'd accept some battering and bruising because that was the kind of heart she had.

But if you broke it, you were history.

That was a nightmare he'd faced when he inadvertently did that ten years ago. He didn't know he'd delivered that blow. He'd considered it since he found out, whether or not he should have said what he said to slow down her pursuit of him so they could both get the wild out before they connected.

The answer he'd come up with was...no. He shouldn't have said it.

It tore him up to know how deeply he'd hurt her.

He didn't know what he should have done in that situation, because, fuck knew, they both needed to get the wild out, and since he wanted her as badly as she wanted him, it was hard as fuck to put her off.

He just wished like hell whatever he said hadn't hurt her.

She spoke, taking him out of these thoughts and reminding him what was most important in the now.

She'd let him back in.

She'd made him work for it, but that was something he had no regrets about at all. He'd do it for longer. He'd relive it. Even if it wasn't much fun the first time, he wouldn't hesitate if it meant she'd be where she was right now.

"So it *is* a secondary command central," she breathed as she looked at the monitors, computers, tech equipment, gun safes and piles of tactical gear. She turned to him. "Do you command legions of mercenaries in bloody coups from here?"

He chuckled. "No."

She appeared disappointed.

He'd given it enough time.

That time was up.

He got in her space and circled her with his arms.

Her sweet tits rested against his chest as she relaxed into him.

Yup. Totally, her tits were high up on his list.

"What you see is the beta version of Nightingale Investigations," he explained. "I didn't have an office when I started, it all ran from here."

"Whoa," she breathed, also circling him with her arms, natural, easy, like they'd done it for more than the few weeks they'd been together.

It felt good.

The wait was over.

That was even better.

And he liked the look on her face. Like she'd just received a precious gift from him, knowing this part of his history, his life.

So yeah.

Oh yeah.

He loved her expressive face.

"Most of this is going to be recycled," he shared. "It's out of date, and it wasn't top of the line when I bought it, because I couldn't afford it then. The setup in the offices is the best you can buy. This has been wired into the surveillance room since I got the office, so I could work from home if I wanted to, but I rarely do that. Since it's rare, there's no need to have a space like this at our place. So it's time for it to go."

"If it's essentially just a home office, why did you keep it locked down?"

"First, because there are weapons in here. They're in safes, but I'm responsible for them, so I'll use every measure of security at hand to keep them as safe as they can be."

She nodded. "Makes sense."

"Second, because even if this equipment is old, it's still worth a whack. It's not like the door is made of steel, but any lock slows down anyone. I have a security system. If someone breached this condo, it might give me thirty more seconds, or three more minutes for them to get through this door. But time is time, and the more you have, the more it's on your side."

"That makes sense too."

He smiled at her.

"Is that why you're here? You're cleaning it out?" she asked.

"Yeah."

"Is there some reason you didn't tell me you were coming here to clean this out?" she asked, which was a turnabout, something she was good at, far better than lying.

The way she asked that, it was on him why he was there and hadn't told her, when they were not one of those couples who shared every move they made during their time apart (unless there was a possibility of snipers setting up for a shot, which, thankfully, was a zone Indy had cleared a few weeks ago). Instead of it being on her, when she had no reason to be there at all, except to break and enter into his defunct home office.

"Got word the place rented this morning," Lee said. "Decided to hit it rather than procrastinate, because tomorrow, you might get kidnapped again. Or you and Ally might get arrested for trying to sneak backstage at the Red Hot Chili Peppers concert, and I'll have to drop everything to wade into that."

Her eyes got big. "The Peppers are in town?"

Noting she seemed unconcerned about future mayhem, considering creating mayhem was her way, even before the recent intensifying of it, but it was concerning to Lee, he looked to the ceiling in search of deliverance.

As usual, he found none.

He dropped his eyes to hers again and tightened his arms. "No trying to sneak backstage."

"I wouldn't do that," she lied. She totally would because she totally already had. "With all the drama recently, I didn't know they were coming to town. I don't have tickets."

Yet was left unsaid.

She shifted her hands so they curled on his shoulders.

"Good news the condo rented," she said quietly.

"Yeah," he replied in the same tone.

"You want me to help you clear this out?"

"Bobby and Matt will clear it out. I'm just sortin' through it, and you can't help with that."

She tipped her head to the side, and he felt her hair slide along his forearms.

Her thick, wild, auburn hair, also high up on his list.

"Want me to hang with you while you sort it?" she offered.

He wanted something from her, and he started backing her to the desk to get it.

The blue in her eyes shimmered in that way he liked so fucking much, and he felt it in his dick.

Also on his list.

"That isn't going to get your stuff sorted, honey," she whispered.

He lifted her so her ass was on the desk, then forced his way in, her knees opening to allow it. "You're with me, so you can't get kidnapped. Seems I got some free time."

She smiled at him.

Definitely at the top of the list.

Indy Savage's smile.

As much as he liked it, Lee angled his head and kissed it off her face.

They were in his Crossfire on the way to a late lunch.

He didn't get much sorting done, but they say even the busiest people needed to carve out time to find ways to de-stress, and he'd definitely checked that off his to-do list.

Indy flipped her phone closed and told him what he knew, since he listened to her side of the conversation. "We have Chowleena duty tomorrow. Both Tod and Stevie are on flights."

"Gotcha."

"We should get a dog."

"If you want a dog, we'll get a dog."

Surprise filtered through the Crossfire.

She processed that quickly and kept going in order to further feel her way through it.

"You should come with me to the Chili Peppers concert. If I can get us tickets."

"That'd be good."

"Ally, obviously, has to come with us."

"Obviously."

More surprise.

This was because, she knew he knew Indy plus Ally plus live rock and roll was not an experience any man, including one who'd been fired on during a variety of iffy occasions, would willingly walk into. He'd learned that the hard way at a Nine Inch Nails concert several years before.

But at his condo he'd come hard, as he always did with Indy.

She'd learn, and she was learning.

Naked gratitude went both ways.

Indy, being Indy, though, pushed it.

"Will you teach me how to pick locks?"

"No."

"Ugh. You're no fun."

He was fun enough half an hour ago.

On that memory, Lee smiled at the windshield as he searched for a parking spot outside Las Delicias.

Not much searching had to be done. There was one right outside the door.

"You and parking spots," Indy remarked as he backed in. "It's unnatural."

"What?" he asked.

"Nothing," she mumbled.

He parked. They got out, went into the restaurant, slid in their booth and ordered without looking at their menus.

Indy was sipping her Diet Coke, Lee his iced tea, and he was reflecting on how much he enjoyed three full weeks of no high-speed chases, car bombs exploding, or dead bodies propped in the doorway of his woman's place of business, when it happened.

"Oh. My. *God*," Indy bit off.

Lee felt her vibe and aimed his gaze from the bowl of chips to over her shoulder, something she was doing too, toward the front door.

"Shit," he muttered.

"She's coming over here!" Indy hissed.

And she was.

Cherry Blackwell, his ex.

She was not a woman he liked. She'd tried to trap him with a baby, something which wasn't conducive to a copacetic breakup.

She was talented in certain areas, but mostly a bitch.

More recently, he didn't like her because she'd confronted Indy and her posse at Twin Dragons. No reason for her to do it. Lee and Cherry had been over for years.

That was just total bitch.

Lee didn't like failure. He took great pains to avoid it.

He considered his attraction to Cherry Blackwell a failure.

It was true, she hid the fact she was a complete bitch from him, because she liked him.

That didn't negate the fact he'd missed it, and that wasn't his style.

"Cherry, don't," he warned low when she stopped at their table.

Though, he had to wince. There were still-healing shrapnel scores on her face.

Cherry didn't listen to him, which presented evidence as to why he'd been with her.

She had attitude. She didn't simper or give into everything he wanted because she wanted him. Both he found boring, and both were surefire that he wouldn't stick around.

Mostly, though, he never got deep with anyone because he was timing his move on Indy.

But Cherry did play games, he just caught it too late.

"*You got me exploded!*" she shrieked at Indy.

Immediately, Lee slid out of the booth. "Cherry, calm down."

She whirled on him. "Fuck calm, Lee. Your *bitch* got me *exploded!* My car is a total write-off, and *look at me!*" she screeched, pointing both hands, fingers straight, nails perfectly manicured, to her face.

In that moment, he gave zero shits about the cuts on her face, the fact he knew she was in the hospital for burn treatment for three days, the fact she probably was still healing in a variety of places on her body now covered with clothes, or the pain all that caused. Even after she'd pulled the shit on him that she'd pulled, he cared when her car exploded, after it exploded, and when she walked toward them moments ago.

Now, he didn't think about it.

He also gave zero shits that, with Cherry being loud, people were turning to watch.

Something clicked, and when that something clicked, there was no way to turn it off.

That something being about Indy, it'd take an act of God to turn it off.

Therefore, Lee got close to Cherry, bent his head to look down at her, and growled, "What did you call my woman?"

"Lee," Indy said soothingly, and he sensed her movement to get out of the booth.

He turned only his head to her. "Stop moving."

For once, she didn't talk back, just stared at him with big eyes and ceased all movement.

He shifted his attention again to Cherry. "Do you know me?"

In the face of his mood, something that could make grown men quake, she was trying to keep her shit together and put on a brave face, but he could see the apprehension in her eyes.

It came out in her voice too. "Y-yes."

"So you know, you do not walk up to my woman and talk shit, you do not call her names, not in front of me, not ever, Cherry. Are you hearing me?"

Cherry took a slight step back.

Lee didn't move, but he did demand, "Answer."

She tried that little-girl pleading he hated so fucking much when he was with her.

Christ, she was a total fail.

"Lee, she got my car exploded."

"Indy might not be your biggest fan, but she had nothin' to do with what happened to you. She might not have the scabs to prove it, but she went through worse than you, Cherry. Far worse. And she isn't traipsing around town gettin' up in people's shit. For fuck's sake, grow up. Or at least learn the world doesn't revolve around you and you can't behave however you like wherever you are. Not when doin' it is selfish, ugly, spiteful and mean. Trust me, babe, it is *not* a good look."

She assumed an expression like he'd slapped her.

Their server, completely ignoring the situation (they were regulars, but even so, nothing got in the way of food being delivered at Las Delicias), landed their order on the table and took off.

As for Lee, he ignored the look on Cherry's face. She'd earned his words, and if she didn't know it with the shit she pulled the last time they were together, she wasn't going to walk away not knowing she'd earned them now.

"Go. Get out of our space," he ordered. "But mark me, Cherry, if I hear Indy or Ally or any of their posse has any problems with you in the future, I won't be happy."

She looked like she was going to say something, wisely decided against it, turned stiltedly, and tried to go for casual as she walked away, but she didn't manage it.

She also didn't look at Indy as she did this, so Lee figured she got his message.

Then again, when that switch was flipped, not many people missed his message.

He slid into the booth and turned to his woman to see if she was okay.

The second he did, he had her hand in his face, and as she forked burrito into her mouth with her other hand, she spoke into her phone, which was tucked to her ear with her head tipped to the side to hold it to her shoulder.

"Ally," she said with a full mouth, then swallowed. "*You will not believe what just happened!*"

She was okay.

Lee unwrapped his own silverware and listened to her tell the story. He sighed through part of it, ate through the rest of it.

When she was done, Indy gave Ally the chance to respond, then cried, "I know! It was totally righteous!"

That was when Lee smiled.

After he finished, but was rolling through the residue of his orgasm, Indy, who'd already had hers (two of them), slid down so he was fully encased and dropped her forehead to his shoulder so her hair slid all over his neck and chest.

They were in lotus position, and he tightened his hold on her, which was already tight.

She turned her head and pressed it against the side of his neck.

"Love you," she whispered, so soft, it was good he had excellent hearing.

"Love you too," he whispered back, not nearly as soft, and slanted his head to tell her what he wanted.

She gave it to him, her mouth.

He kissed her as he shifted her to her back, him on top.

When he stopped kissing her, he lifted his head and looked down at her through the shadows of her darkened bedroom.

When they got married, started a family, they'd have to move. It'd suck. He'd been coming to this duplex for as long as he could remember. It reminded him of Grandma Ellen, a woman always full of vibrancy and energy and love. And now it was all about Indy, who was all of the same.

But it was too small for a family.

However, even when they moved, he was giving Indy a free hand to decorate their bedroom.

This room was her. The real her. All woman. The power of the feminine. Having it and flaunting it. But there was a delicacy to it.

Her hidden core. The softness. The sweetness. The vulnerability she refused to show, except to the man who she let sleep at her side.

And that was powerful too.

He felt like an invader in this room. He'd worked hard for the honor of being in her bed.

It was part of the spoils of winning India Savage.

He'd wanted her since he knew what girls could be to boys.

Now she was his.

And he didn't ever want to lose that feeling.

"Is there a second wave of people you need to call to tell what happened with Cherry?" he teased.

She'd been on the phone all afternoon. He might be wrong, but he thought she'd even made a call to a friend in England.

"Not exactly," she returned. "But there will be follow up that's necessary to bask in the afterglow."

He grinned at her through the dark.

With the sudden change in her vibe, Lee knew what was coming when she rested her hand on his cheek and swept her thumb over his lips.

"Those marks on her face—" she began, her voice now quiet, concern threading through it.

And there was the softness.

The sweetness.

The real Indy.

Absolutely at the top of his list.

Even so.

"You're not responsible," he replied firmly.

"Her car exploded, Lee."

"You're still not responsible."

"I know, but—"

"I get it. Wilcox isn't available for her to be mad at, but that doesn't mean she gets to take her shit out on you. You didn't plant that bomb. You also didn't walk up to her while she was enjoying a night out with her girls and say nasty shit to her or in front of her mother. Honest to God, if that car bomb hadn't happened, and she walked into LD and saw us, what do you think she'd do?"

"Come over to visit and spread her brand of bitchy cheer all over our burritos."

"Exactly."

"No one should mess with an LD burrito," she mumbled.

"Gorgeous," he called tersely to get her complete attention.

"What?"

"It sucks that happened to her. But if you don't learn your lesson not to be a total asshole after rollin' around in hot and sour soup, when your car explodes, you learn. If you don't, it's fair game how those lessons are taught. I don't suspect today's gonna turn her into Mother Theresa, but maybe it'll have penetrated, even a little bit."

"I'm not sure. Cherry has pretty fortified bitch defenses."

Lee started chuckling, even if that was true.

"I mean, what she did to you," she continued. "It was pretty ballsy she went on the offensive at all, considering your history."

"Agreed."

"Are you...over that?"

"I didn't knock her up, fortunately, so I was over it after I finished things with her. But I don't want to have to buy an industrial washing machine to clean your clothes should there be a next go 'round with you and her. Denver is a big city. But it isn't big enough for the two of you if she doesn't back off."

"It wasn't me who threw the soup," she informed him.

"Whatever," he muttered.

"It wasn't." That was more heated.

Lee sighed. "Honey, can this be the last time Cherry is in our bed?"

She gave that a second to mull over, then agreed. "Absolutely."

He kissed her quick then pulled them both out of bed so they could do the sex clean up and hit it to actually sleep.

He had her pinned mostly under him in bed, the soft drone of traffic on Broadway one block away acting as their white noise, and he was close to drifting off. He already thought she had, when she mumbled sleepily, "I forgot to tell you. Ally texted while I was talking to Marianne. She scored some tickets to RHCP."

Well...

Shit.

At least whatever he was in for wouldn't be boring.

And fuck him, he'd never admit it, not out loud, but whatever it was, he was looking forward to it.

Because it would be pure Indy.

Lee settled deeper into his woman.

And he fell asleep.

TRACK 2
ROCK CHICK RESCUE

Show Her

Eddie

Eddie let himself into the kitchen through the back door.

He did not smell what he normally smelled; some of Jet's amazing cooking.

He immediately smelled paint.

"*Mi amor?*" he called.

Nothing.

He moved farther into the house. "Jet?"

Still nothing.

She wasn't in the living room, so he headed to the hall.

And he stopped dead at the door to the bathroom.

It was painted.

Purple.

It was a deep, dark purple. If there was a shade of purple that was a modicum of masculine, this was it.

It was still purple.

"Jet!" he shouted, thinking maybe she was downstairs doing the laundry and having a few things to say about a purple bathroom.

That day, she'd taken off from Fortnum's. Her plans were to get her hair done and run some errands.

There had been no mention of painting the bathroom, and absolutely no mention of painting it purple.

But she wasn't at home.

Her car was in the garage. He'd just parked next to that piece of shit.

It had only been a couple of months since he'd dropped a load on getting it running.

It was still a piece of shit.

His woman needed a new car.

Bad.

When he received no answer, a frisson he didn't like slithered through his frame, and he pulled out his phone.

Since it'd happened, he'd tried, but he couldn't get that last scene with Jet and Vince Fratelli out of his head.

On one hand, he'd trust his life to Lee. He knew, logically, that his *hermano* had the situation under control.

On the other hand, it had happened to Jet, and with her, his logic flew out the window.

Not to mention, when her ordeal was over, he'd come home to a house that was sparkling clean, and her shit was gone.

He'd sorted that right fucking quick, but the Rock Chicks had a way of finding trouble.

It had been weeks, the shit with Hank and Roxie had come and gone, Roxie was in Chicago preparing to move back, all seemed calm.

But Eddie still didn't like the fact he was home, Jet's car was in the garage, and she wasn't answering his call.

Jet's shit had been worse than Indy's.

Roxie's had been worse than Jet's.

If this kept going, he didn't know how he was going to handle it.

One way he knew would help was if all the shit stopped happening to Jet.

But she was supposed to be home, and she was not.

And he didn't like that.

Before he could call her again, his phone rang, and the screen said, Jet Calling.

He took the call by saying, "Where the fuck are you?"

"Eddie?"

Oh fuck.

He knew what the sound of *that* "Eddie" meant.

"Where are you?" he demanded.

"Lavonne and Bear's."

This seemed innocuous, but since her father was staying at Lavonne and Bear's, he knew it was not.

"And, um, Indy's here with me," she went on hesitantly.

Indy. Wildcard, with an emphasis on wild.

"Give it all to me, *chiquita*," he ordered.

"And mom and Lottie. And, um…Tex."

He turned on his boot and retraced his steps to the door, asking, "Do I need grenades?"

"Probably not…" More hesitation, then, "but maybe a call to Lee wouldn't be remiss."

Fuck.

When he got to the house, a house he'd only been to once and he'd never been inside, he walked in without knocking.

He was momentarily stunned at what he saw.

The yard was a disaster. It looked like Chernobyl twenty years post-meltdown.

But the inside was neat as a pin, countrified so much it made him appreciate his new purple bathroom, and choked in hearts.

Eddie only allowed this to momentarily take his attention, because what he took in next, he didn't get.

First, Jet seemed fine. She was standing next to her dad, and both looked fit. No one was bleeding, and he might miss it from the stale (and fresh) cigarette odor that clogged the air, but he couldn't smell any expended gunpowder.

Indy was sitting next to Tex on a couch. They were eating from a bucket of chicken wings. Tex had hot sauce all over his mustache and beard. Indy did not.

Lottie was in an armchair. She was doing her nails.

What seemed to be the problem was Bear appeared to be facing off against Lavonne...and Nancy.

Nancy looking pissed was probably why Tex was there. Or Nancy being there at all was why Tex was.

But Nancy wasn't prone to getting pissed, and when it happened, it was usually on someone else's behalf.

Even if there didn't seem to be any immediate danger, Eddie didn't let his guard down. Bear was probably in his mid to late fifties. If he'd ever attempted to stay in shape, that was a thing of the past, that past being decades ago. Nevertheless, the man was enormous, and bulk could be dangerous if the person who had it knew how to use it.

Eddie had already clocked the guy as knowing how to use it.

Lavonne was small, but wiry, and Eddie figured when she was riled, she was like a rabid chihuahua that could take down a pit bull.

He pinned Jet with his eyes.

"*Cariño?*" he called.

She came to him, put her hand on his chest and looked up in his eyes.

On her way, he would have liked to appreciate the snug sweater she wore, the tight jeans and the high-heeled boots that did great things to a naturally perfect ass. Not to mention, she had seen Trixie at her salon that day, so her hair was freshly highlighted and styled, with that sexy-as-all-fuck sweep of bangs across her eyes that was now even sexier.

The look she wore on her face, he didn't take the time to appreciate any of it.

"Talk to me," he demanded.

"Okay. See, Mom and Lottie were just over to visit Lavonne, you know, girl chat and—"

"Jet," he grunted in order to get her to focus.

"So *annnnnyyyywaaaaay*..." she trailed off but did it turning to give big eyes to her father.

Eddie's attention cut to Ray.

"Ray?" he bit off.

Ray put up both hands. "Don't look at me."

"Oh for fuck's sake," Tex boomed, then using a partially-gnawed-on chicken wing, he pointed at Lavonne. "She..." He swung the wing to Bear, "Wants him out. He..." He whirled the wing in the air. "Won't leave. I don't know what the big deal is and why Jet had to call in the fuzz."

Eddie also didn't have the time to react to Tex using the term "the fuzz."

He'd come home from work, expecting to eat dinner with his woman, watch TV with her, fuck her, then sleep beside her.

Instead, he got a purple bathroom and a callout to Chernobyl house.

He looked down at Jet and raised his brows.

"I think she's worried about this," Lavonne put in at that juncture.

Eddie's gaze went to her, and his body went solid, because she was squinting through the smoke drifting up from the cigarette between her lips and brandishing a long-barrel .44 Magnum revolver.

"Yeah," Jet whispered. "That's what I'm worried about."

Eddie's voice was such a quick lash, Lavonne jumped when he ordered, "Put that down."

She squinted harder at Eddie, deciding something, then she made the wrong decision.

"You get his lazy ass outta my house, I'll put this down."

He heard the door open behind him but didn't turn to it, knowing it was Lee, since he called him on his way over. Instead, he stalked across the room and wrenched the weapon from the woman's hand.

"Hey!" she shouted, the cigarette hovering on her lower lip, but either by a miracle or through practice, it held.

"What's goin' on?" he heard Lee ask behind him.

"This isn't a toy," Eddie snarled at Lavonne.

She plucked the smoke out of her mouth and retorted, "I know it's not a toy. I also know I want his good-for-nothin' ass out of my house, and he ain't goin'."

"It's my house too!" Bear yelled.

Lavonne leaned to the side to see around Eddie and asked her husband, "Oh yeah? When's the last time you put money in the bank to pay the mortgage? Hunh? When's the last time you even sat your lazy ass down to write out the check to pay the mortgage? *Hunh?*"

Bear flung an arm toward Ray. "I gotta look after my boy here."

Ray—who'd had a clean bill of health delivered to him at his last doctor's visit, but who had been putting a fair amount of effort into getting on with his life for weeks, doing this like he was a man on a mission, something Eddie suspected happened when someone stabbed you repeatedly, shot you and threw you from a moving vehicle so your daughter could deal with the literal bloody mess you'd made of your life—took a step back, put his hands up again and said, "I'm not in this."

"No, you're not," Lavonne agreed. "'Cause you're bein' good. Goin' to meetin's. Got yourself a job. Givin' me money I didn't even ask for to cover that food I put in your belly and that bed you sleep in. Gettin' your shit together. You know who's not gettin' their shit together?" She poked her finger at Bear but turned accusing eyes to Eddie. "It packs a bigger punch when I do that with my .44."

"God, I missed home," Lottie remarked fondly, and when Eddie glanced at her, he saw she said it while stroking the brush on a nail and not looking up from her task. "So glad to be back."

"And we sure are glad to have you back, hon," Lavonne said fondly.

Fuck him.

Eddie turned his attention to Jet.

She bit her lip and shrugged her shoulders.

"Eddie already disarmed her, took the fun out of it, if you ask me," Tex put in, aiming this at Lee. "So you're overkill."

Lee locked eyes with Eddie, and Eddie knew his friend felt his pain.

"Eddie," Nancy said quietly.

He twisted at the waist to look at Jet's mom.

With what he saw, he twisted back and said to Bear, "You need to find somewhere else to sleep tonight."

"Huh," Lavonne grunted victoriously.

"I ain't goin'," Bear declared stubbornly.

That was when Tex lost interest in his chicken wings. He tossed some picked-clean bones on a heart-shaped plate Lavonne had set out for them on the coffee table and stood to his very tall, massively bulky height.

He leveled his gaze on Bear and said, "Nancy wants you gone 'cause Lavonne wants you gone, which means you're gone, turkey."

"I barely even *know* you. You're not gonna tell me what to do in my own damned house," Bear shot back.

That was when Tex lifted one long, beefy leg and stepped over the coffee table like it was a small fallen branch.

Bear was smart enough to back up, but not smart enough, because he didn't back far enough, like, out the door.

Shit.

Now they had a situation.

Eddie and Lee closed in.

Ray, too, got closer.

"Pack a bag, brother," Ray said carefully to Bear.

Bear didn't take his eyes off Tex as he crossed his arms on his chest. "Not goin'.'"

"You're out or I put you out," Tex warned.

"I'd like to see you try," Bear returned.

Tex grinned, hot sauce glistening, and even Eddie felt a shiver because the man looked deranged. Or, more deranged than normal.

Ray shifted so he was between Tex and Bear, his back to Tex.

"C'mon, Bear. Talk to Lavonne later when she cools down," he urged.

"Not gonna cool down this time," Lavonne called.

Eddie watched Ray's head tip slightly to the side and the look that crossed his face that said without words, *You've heard that before, give her what she wants, this will blow over.*

Bear made them wait a few beats before it was him doing the leaning to stare down Lavonne.

"Not gonna forget anytime soon you pointin' that .44 at me, woman," he threatened.

She took a drag from her cigarette, blew out the smoke, and replied, "Good."

Bear made a face at her, swept the room with his gaze without catching on anyone, turned and stormed down the hall.

"Not as good as car bombs, but it'll do," Tex mumbled as he lumbered back to the couch and his bucket of wings.

Nancy giggled.

Eddie caught Jet's eyes and blew out a sigh.

They stopped at Famous on the way home to get a pizza for dinner.

Not as good as Jet's meatloaf or her chili, but then, nothing was.

She made up for it by scooping out a treat she'd introduced him to shortly after her shit settled. Vanilla bean ice cream with a huge wodge of chunky peanut butter slopped on, this smothered in chocolate sauce.

Since he wasn't about to get a gut, he decided they'd need to be energetic to work it off.

And how he chose them to do it, he didn't mind he was doing most of the work.

Though, his woman put a fair amount in herself.

She was taking it doggie-style, one of her arms out, hand braced to the headboard so the effort he was expending didn't get lost in the sway, at the same time giving herself an anchor to meet him, when he heard that sweet catch in her throat.

He pulled out, she made a new noise, one that told him she didn't like that, but she got over it when he rolled her to her back, swung her leg in front of him and hiked her up his thighs, pounding back in.

He watched her take him, and Christ, she was pretty.

She also needed to blow.

He shifted a thumb between her legs and saw to that.

After that was accomplished, he let go.

He lowered himself to her after his orgasm left him, and she wound her limbs around him.

He felt that, where she had hold of him, on the outside and on the inside.

This woman loved him. This woman, with her snug tops and perfect ass and sexy bangs and phenomenal cooking skills and beautiful smile and huge heart, loved him.

But...

"Purple?" he asked.

Her body tightened underneath him, so he smoothed a hand down her side, her hip, and then up to cup her breast.

"Do you hate it?"

"Is Prince coming for a visit?"

She giggled and, better, relaxed.

She had her mother's gorgeous smile.

She also had her mother's giggle.

He moved his hand from her tit to her neck. "There's one good thing about the bathroom."

"What's that?"

"I didn't have to paint it."

A laugh this time, not a giggle, but he'd take it.

"You like it?" he asked softly.

"I think it looks amazing," she said timidly, and that was his woman too. She was shy. She was losing that with him, but she loved him. She wanted him to like his bathroom. She worried.

If he didn't like it, she'd paint it again tomorrow, he knew it.

He didn't hate it, and as he said, he didn't have to do it himself, so he knew he could live with it.

"Then I like it," he only slightly lied.

"Good," she whispered.

"How'd you do that and get your hair done today?"

"Stevie and Duke came over to help."

"Ah."

"And it's a small room."

"Right."

"She'll take him back."

Now she'd lost him.

"What?"

"Lavonne. She'll take Bear back. She always does."

"Not my problem, not yours. Unless you're in the line of fire when she's waving around a revolver."

"There's nothing fun about watching people fight, but I'll admit, that made it a whole lot less fun."

Considering Jet had been in that room, and it had concerned her enough to call him, Eddie started to get pissed.

Jet covered his hand at her neck and said gently, "It's over."

His voice was inflexible when he said, "That was far from cool."

"Agreed, but I noticed you didn't give it back to her when we left, so it won't happen again."

No, he didn't. And he wouldn't. You didn't use a firearm to put strength behind a threat when you were bickering with your spouse. You used it for protection. The end.

But he wasn't going to discuss that with Jet.

"It was sweet, when Tex saw Mom was over it and he waded in."

"You need to prepare, *mi amor*, he's in deep for her."

He said it even knowing he didn't have to. Jet adored Tex. In the short time the man had been in her life, he'd been a better father to her, and a better partner to Nancy, than Ray had in her twenty-eight years.

But the stillness he felt in her was not about what he said.

It was about what he hadn't yet said.

She loved him, he knew it, she showed it with peanut butter and chocolate sauce sundaes, and a fuckuva lot more.

She'd also told him.

He hadn't told her.

He felt the same. It was there. He knew it when he saw the empty space where her bag used to be when she tried to break up with him after her ordeal.

But before he gave it to her, he needed them to have more than a couple of weeks under their belts.

They had that now.

She had to know.

He had a purple bathroom, and he didn't throw a shit fit.

He came home from work only to have to haul his ass to Lakewood to extricate her from a situation that involved a .44.

But he wasn't going to tell her. Not now.

She wouldn't believe him.

Ray seemed to be turning his life around, but he'd been a shit dad and a shit husband who'd left his woman and daughters with serious baggage.

Eddie had more work to do to show her, and he was down to put in that work, as long as it took.

And when the time was right, she'd have the words.

"I know," she replied belatedly about what he said about Tex, maybe waiting for Eddie to say what he hoped they both knew. Maybe not.

But since it wasn't time, he moved them past it.

He touched his mouth to hers then asked, "Ready to go to sleep?"

He watched her nod on the pillow.

He grinned, saw her eyes drop to where he knew his dimple was, and they warmed. The love blasted out of them, and Eddie decided it wasn't time to sleep.

Not yet.

Later.

They had more business to see to.

But this time, it wasn't about the fact he had ice cream to work off.

"Oh my God, *stop doing this!*" Jet cried as he hauled her out of bed the next morning.

"You like our showers," he reminded her as, hands to her hip with her in front of him, he guided their way to the bathroom. "Why you always bitch about it, I have no clue."

She turned in his hold and stood firm, so he "had to" bump into her. He then took the opportunity to stay close.

"Do they have to happen at five thirty in the morning?" she demanded.

"Yes."

She heaved a huge sigh that was cute, and which had the added benefit of pushing her tits against his chest.

After he enjoyed that, he whipped her around, replaced his hands on her hips and took her to their purple bathroom.

Jet was at his side. She had heels to her chair, thighs to her chest, the chair angled away from the table and facing him sitting at its head, and she was munching toast and staring at him.

Eddie swallowed the eggs she'd made him and advised, "*Chiq-uita*, give it up. We're gonna fool around every morning in the shower until I croak at age eighty-nine."

Her lips parted, her eyes went huge, but she said nothing.

Show her.

Right, so that wasn't showing as much as telling.

Though, the shower was definitely showing.

When he didn't follow that up, she threw her toast on the plate, swiped her hands above it to get rid of the crumbs, then refocused on him.

"Eddie, I'm all right."

He smiled at her. "Know that, *cariño*. You're vocal."

She rolled her eyes and said, "I know this is hard, given the certain appendage you have that makes it always on your mind, but I'm not talking about sex."

He forked up more eggs. "What are you talking about?"

"You toss and turn in your sleep, and sometimes grab me...really hard."

Fork halfway to his mouth, Eddie froze, eyes to Jet. "*Cómo?*"

She reacted to his tone, his intensity, he knew it because her voice went soft when she shared, "You don't hurt me."

He put his fork down, sat back and gave her his full attention. "Tell me."

"Since that night, since...Vince, it happens. Not every night. But often enough, and it's not going away," she explained. She put her feet down, leaned to him and wrapped her hand on his forearm resting on the table. "Baby, I'm all right."

"I know you are," he said shortly. "I grab you? Hard?"

She squeezed his arm while shaking her head. "Like I said, it doesn't hurt."

"Why don't you wake me?"

She looked confused. "Because you have an important job. You need your sleep."

Christ.

His woman.

"*Cariño*, I grab you hard and I'm unconscious, you wake me so I don't hurt you not knowin' I'm hurtin' you."

"You grab me harder when we're having sex. Obviously, I don't mind that," she teased.

Teasing wasn't going to work.

Not this time.

No fucking way.

"I want you to wake me."

"I'm not going to wake you."

"Jet."

"Eddie."

"*Jet*," he bit off.

"*Eddie*," she mimicked him.

"This isn't funny," he gritted.

"I know it's not. I also know he can't hurt me. He's dead. If you're still angry with Lee, work it out with Lee. If you're angry with me, work it out with me."

"I'm not angry with you."

"Do you normally toss and turn in your sleep?"

"I don't know. I'm sleeping."

"You didn't before Vince."

Eddie pulled from her hold, returned his attention to his plate, picking up his fork, and clipped, "Stop saying his fucking name."

"Eddie."

He knew that "Eddie" too. It was, "listen to me, I'm worried about you, Eddie."

But fuck that.

He tossed his fork on his plate, sat back again, and exploded, "*He had your pants undone!*"

Jet held his gaze, said nothing, but didn't back down or away.

"Jesus fucking Christ, he had your pants undone," he continued. "He had his hands on you. You were scared. Nope. You were terrified."

She said something to that. "Lee had it contained."

"I don't give a fuck," he returned. "And you didn't know that at the time, or you wouldn't have been terrified."

"I'm fine," she said quietly.

"*I know that*," he barked.

She held his gaze again. A beat passed. Two.

Then she got up, came to him, and he tipped his head to keep his eyes on her.

She put her hands on him, smoothing his hair back, not taking her attention from his face. Eventually, she just held the sides of his head before she bent and touched her lips to his.

When she straightened, she mumbled, "You'll work it out in your own time." She let him go, turned, nabbed her coffee cup and asked, "Want more coffee?"

That was when he was up and had her in his arms, her back molded to his front, his face in her neck.

She gave him that, sliding her hands along his arms so she was holding him while he held her.

Then she whispered, "It's over, honey."

"Yeah," he grunted into her neck.

"Do you want more coffee?"

"Yeah."

"Are you sure you're not mad about the bathroom?"

He laughed in her skin, kissed her there, and at her ear, repeated, "Yeah."

She turned her head, he lifted his, and they caught eyes.

"Give me your mug, Eddie."

I love the fuck out of you, he thought, staring into her eyes.

Same, she thought back, staring into his.

After they shared that, he kissed her mouth, let her go and gave Jet his mug.

TRACK 3
ROCK CHICK REDEMPTION

Her Man

Hank

Hank woke without woman or dog.

And he didn't like it.

He opened his eyes, got up on his forearm and listened to the house.

Only then did a smile curve his lips.

They were in the kitchen.

He grabbed the covers, threw them off, snatched his pajama bottoms from the floor and headed to the bathroom. After taking care of business, wearing the bottoms, he was leaving the bathroom just as Roxie and Shamus walked into the bedroom.

She was carrying a tray he'd never seen before. It had little legs on it, and from what he could smell, on the plate on top, there was bacon.

She was also wearing a dark-gray sleep dress that hugged her curves and fell to her ankles. It had long sleeves that fit close and a notch on a collar that dipped down to expose her collarbone.

He had no idea how she managed to make a winter nightdress sexy, but one thing his woman found easy to do: make pretty much anything sexy.

Shamus danced to Hank.

Roxie glared at him. "You're up!"

He grinned at her and pointed out the obvious. "Yeah."

"I can't serve you breakfast in bed when you're not *in* the bed," she informed him.

Fighting a smile, he gave his dog's head a rubdown before he sauntered to the bed, adjusted the pillows and then reclined, straightening his legs.

She plopped the tray over his thighs.

And yeah, there was bacon.

Also, his favorite. Roxie's stuffed French toast, the pat of butter still melting and mixing with an overabundance of maple syrup poured over the top, just as he liked it.

She'd been with him now for a while. Through her drama, them being separated while she dealt with moving to Denver (a time he didn't like all that much, the primary reason why he'd colluded with Tex to get her to move right in with him when she returned, an endeavor that was thankfully a success), then Roxie coming home, moving in with him and them surviving the most recent drama.

Barely.

Now, they were back to normal.

He liked Roxie beside him in his life and his bed a whole fuckuva lot. He liked walking his dog with her. He liked looking at her and listening to her. He liked going to the movies with her and going to the grocery store with her. He liked coming home to her. He liked seeing her face light up when he walked into the house and cooking dinner with her and watching TV with her and listening to her when he made her laugh. He even liked being her rock when shit went south with the Rock Chicks.

He just liked her.

But he liked their normal the best.

Like now.

She rounded the bed and hiked up the bottom of her nightdress exposing shapely legs all the way up to her thighs (again, sexy).

She climbed in opposite him, then said a gentle, "Shamus, no, not this time. Daddy's eating," when their dog tried to climb in too.

Shamus whined.

"I'm sorry, baby," she cooed. "He'll be done soon and then you can come up."

Right, and he liked how much she loved his dog, and how much Shamus loved her too.

Though she was correct, he would be done with his breakfast soon (Roxie's French toast never lasted long before he downed it), but Shamus wouldn't be getting on the bed when he was finished.

It was Saturday. For once in the Rock Chick World, they not only had no dramas, they had no plans.

But Hank did, and they heavily involved this bed, so Shamus wasn't invited.

"'Mornin'," he said softly when she finally looked to him.

Her beautiful face warmed, she leaned into him and touched his mouth with hers, pulling away, and after that sweet touch said it all, unnecessarily adding, "Good morning, Whisky."

He gestured to the tray. "None for you?"

"We're sharing. The toast is a double stack."

He looked closer and saw she was right. There were also two forks.

He grabbed one and handed it to her, then went after the other.

But he started with a sip from his coffee.

She dug in. He went in after her.

After he swallowed his first bite and savored it, he turned back to his woman. "New tray?"

"Tod and Stevie and I went shopping yesterday."

This was not a rare occurrence. His woman could shop.

However, it was in overdrive since Christmas was nearly on them.

"Did you buy two?" he asked.

She forked into the French toast then gave him her gaze before she shoved the bite into her mouth. "We only need one."

She was right about that.

It was then Hank leaned in and kissed her. It was closed-mouthed, but she still tasted of Roxie and syrup. The first part did it for him. All he needed. So the combination packed a phenomenal punch.

He put down his fork and picked up a rasher of bacon, saying, "I could get used to this," before he munched.

That was no lie, and he wasn't just talking about sharing breakfast in bed.

He was feeling great. He had his woman at his side, eating a fantastic breakfast, the entire day off, no plans, the house was decorated for Christmas, he was in the spirit, Roxie was in the spirit, Shamus was in the spirit, and no one had been kidnapped or shot for weeks.

So he wasn't feeling great about how Roxie suddenly couldn't meet his eyes.

"Sunshine?" he called.

She looked right at him and said fast, "I tried, but I couldn't stop it."

Oh fuck.

His entire frame tensed.

"What?" he growled.

"It was already done by the time they called. Apparently, they've been planning this for weeks."

"What, Roxanne?" he pressed, his voice still low.

Her eyes got big before she announced, "Mom and Dad are coming for Christmas."

He did a slow blink.

"That's it?" he asked.

"Okay, Hank," she began, scooching closer to him like she had to be near to support him through a trauma. "You had a small taste of them when they were here."

"Sweetheart—"

"And it was Halloween, which is a holiday, I'll admit. So Mom was acting in true form when she Mom Bombed your house in all things Halloween. But you must remember, that isn't *the* holiday. Christmas is."

"Roxie—"

"So, you experienced Mom Overload when she was here around Halloween. And I know I warned you, but I don't think you appreciate just how much Christmas is crazy town for my mom."

Trish Logan, down to the bone, was "crazy town."

But she was also hilarious, loved her daughter, loved Hank with her daughter, and family was family, and it didn't need to be said, Christmas was family time.

"I did promise her Christmases," he reminded her.

"I know, but this year, with things..." she trailed off.

It was hard for her to talk about it.

It was hard for any of them to talk about it.

So he didn't make her talk about it.

"I know," he murmured.

"We had to stay in Denver. For Vance."

Everything was fine now. It was a miracle, but it was.

But she was right. They had to stay in Denver, especially Roxie. For Vance.

"This is about Tex too, I assume," Hank noted.

She nodded. "Mom has him back, and as usual with Mom, she's going for the gusto."

"It's gonna be okay," he assured her.

"It's not going to be okay," she returned.

"Sunshine," he wrapped his hand around her neck, "it's going to be okay."

She searched his eyes. After a few beats, hers settled.

Because that was what he was for her.

Her rock.

She was his everything, and that was what he was for her.

So, yeah.

It was going to be okay.

Because even if it wasn't, he'd make it that way.

"Oh my God!" Roxie yelled from the kitchen.

Luke and Hank, both in the back room watching a football game, looked at each other.

And they both grinned.

Roxie showed in the room and shouted, "I just *knew* I shouldn't let Tex pick them up from the airport!"

After delivering that, she flounced out.

Luke and Hank were buds, but they didn't hang often. Luke was there to be witness to what happened next.

Hank didn't blame him, and he was surprised he didn't have a house full of Rock Chicks and Hank's friends. Trish and Herb's entertainment value was second to none, and it was far better to watch it unfold than to listen to what went down after the fact. (Though, that was good too.)

Both men stood and strolled from the back room into the kitchen where they saw Roxie standing in the open front door, shouting out of it.

"Mom! It's December twenty-third! We already have a tree!"

Hank instantly looked over the kitchen sink out the window.

And sure enough, outside in the freshly fallen snow, Shamus was dancing around Herb and Tex, who were carting in a massive fir tree.

Explaining how that could happen, Tex's El Camino wasn't at the curb. He'd borrowed one of Lee's company Explorers. And it looked piled high in the back with wrapped Christmas presents.

Hank bit back a bark of laughter.

"You can't have too many Christmas trees, Roxanne Giselle," Trish announced reproachfully, right before she pulled her daughter forcefully into her arms and hugged her so tight, you could see how tight it was, doing this while swinging her back and forth.

She then caught sight of Hank, let Roxie go and shoved her aside with such force, Roxie's hair swayed.

She called, "Sweet Jesus! Praise the Lord!" while coming his way.

"Hey there, Trish," he greeted, moving toward her and still holding back laughter.

"Sweet Jesus!" she shouted.

"Not in the house two seconds, and she's covering it in Sweet Jesus," Herb grumbled from the direction of the door as Trish hugged him tight.

"It *is* Christmas, Sweet Jesus seems the way to go," he heard Luke say under his breath.

Hank put a stop to the swaying by standing firm, but he hugged Trish back, and he did it *still* holding back laughter.

She let him go and turned to Luke.

Hank watched with interest to see what happened next. Not many people hugged Luke Stark.

Trish Logan was not many people.

Although Luke didn't reciprocate, Trish wasn't deterred, and even when it was over, she reached up to pat his cheek and mumbled, "You're a good boy."

Luke Stark.

A good boy.

That was too much. Hank was almost certain he sprained something trying not to bust out laughing, but Luke's only response was his lips forming a smirk.

"Trish Logan, I told you, this huge-ass tree ain't gonna fit in this room," Herb announced, standing with Tex in Hank's living room with the tree up and unfurled. He then looked to Hank. "Son," he greeted, his eyes going to Luke. "Luke."

They both said the same thing in reply.

"Herb."

And Herb told no lies. The tree was massive and taking up all the available space. So much, both Tex and Herb were partially obscured by the branches.

Trish was taking off her coat with no apparent concern that there was a probably very expensive tree that could not remain in that house (it also probably couldn't be returned) taking up the living room.

"It's not meant for in here. It's meant for the family room," she declared.

Oh shit.

Hank and Roxie's tree was already set up in the family room. It had been since the weekend after Thanksgiving. It was a beautiful live tree, with all new ornaments, and even if Hank wasn't much of a shopper, he'd enjoyed traipsing from store to store all over Denver with Roxie to find exactly what they wanted.

Roxie, being expert in all the varied retail experiences, took him on this quest weeks before Thanksgiving, because, she shared, she went nowhere near any store on the weekend after Thanksgiving.

"Black Friday and the ensuing weekend are my version of the seventh circle of hell," she'd proclaimed, something Hank thought was damned good to know.

It was a great memory. Drinking hot cocoa and listening to Bing Crosby, Nat King Cole, and the Carpenters' Christmas albums, and setting up the house with his woman had been something he'd never forget. Making love to her under the tree with the smell of pine in his nose and the crooning of Cole in his ears, and Roxie filling all the rest of his senses when they got it all done being the best part.

She hadn't hidden she enjoyed all of that too. There could be no mistake, Trish had handed down her holiday joy to her daughter.

Therefore, as he suspected, and he didn't even need her to shoot the aggravated look she shot to him to suspect it, Roxie waded in at this point. "As I said when you arrived, *Mom*, we already have our tree. And it's in the family room."

"We'll move that one into the living room," Trish returned.

Oh shit...again.

Roxie shot Hank another aggravated look, but the level of aggravation in this one was reaching the red zone.

He tried to be supportive in the one he returned, but he worried he failed, mostly because he thought this was all funny as fuck, including the fact she didn't.

The Roxie and Trish show was almost as good as the Trish and Herb show.

She turned back to her mother. "No, we won't, Mom. Hank and I bought our tree together. We went out and got our decorations together. We also decorated it together. It's our first Christmas together and that tree is *not moving*. We're having Christmas around *that...exact...tree. No discussion*."

The Logan women squared off.

Regrettably, or fortunately, depending on who you were in the scenario, Herb decided to chime in. "No problem, even though this tree cost me more than I'd accept for payment for a donated gonad, I'll take it out back and chop it up. Hank can use it as firewood."

Trish whirled on Herb, horrorstruck. "First, Herbert Logan, do not talk about your gonads in mixed company! Or, say, *at all*. Does your daughter need to hear about your gonads?" Her hand shot up when Herb's mouth opened. "I'll answer that. No! She doesn't. And second, you are *not* chopping up that tree! We'll set it up outside in the front. Put lights on it. It'll be perfect. It'll be the talk of the neighborhood."

"I just hauled it in, now you want me to haul it out?" Herb asked incredulously.

"You were gonna haul it out back to chop it up," Trish pointed out.

"Yeah, but I do that, I get to use an axe. I take it out front, I gotta deal with lights. I already dealt with my quota of Christmas lights this season, woman," Herb warned. Then he continued, doing it quickly so Trish couldn't get a word in, "And you know that since I told you five damn-gummed times after you kept wanting me to staple lights on shit."

Herb looked to Hank and carried on ranting.

"We got lights on the house. The detached garage. The garden shed. The fence around the property. In all the trees. Around the banister out front *and* the one on the stairs *in* the goldarned house. And I know I'm forgettin' some, mostly because, eventually I had to block it out so I wouldn't commit a felonious act, seein' as we got a cop in the family now, and you don't need your girl's father facin' twenty to life for wife-icide."

Definitely sprained something trying not to laugh.

Herb concluded, "*And* she made me do all this knowin' the whole time we weren't even gonna *be* there for Christmas."

Hank moved into the fray, setting off toward the tree. "I'll set it up. Head to Lowe's, get some more lights. It won't be a problem."

"The Lord sure heard my prayers, giving my daughter a *good* and *decent* man who doesn't bellyache at Christmas," Trish decreed. This statement was part snotty, that part directed at Herb, and part heartfelt, that part directed at Hank. She then said while opening the refrigerator, "Don't go to Lowe's just yet, Hank. I might have a grocery list for you."

"Mom," Roxie cut in. "This house is groaning with food. You sprung it on us, but we did have *some* notice you were coming." The stress on the word "some," Hank didn't miss, was pretty heavy. "I got everything we could possibly need yesterday."

"Nothing wrong with me checking," Trish retorted.

Roxie let out a loud sigh.

"Nip this shit in the bud, son," Herb advised as Hank took control of the tree. "She'll have you runnin' all over hell's half acre for her if you don't."

"It's fine," Hank assured and started out the door, catching Tex grinning like a maniac.

Right.

Even if it wasn't already, that made it worth it right there.

Tex was happy his family was in town for the holiday.

Yep.

Totally worth it.

"Oh, and while you're out there..." Trish called, head now in the fridge as Hank was halfway out the door with the tree, "...can you help Herb and Tex with our bags and the packages? We mailed them early to Tex. They're wrapped and everything, so we're all set to start Christmas without delay!" She peered around the fridge door to Luke, "You go too, Lucas. We've got a lot to bring in."

Luke touched his finger to his forehead and flicked it out in a salute before heading toward the front door.

He was still smirking.

"Hell's half acre," Herb grumbled, following Hank out the door. "That's where I live. That's my life."

Hank mentally called bullshit.

Herb doted on his wife.

He bitched a lot, but it hadn't escaped Hank, he gave in.

Every time.

Hank woke without woman or dog.

It was the dead of night.

Christmas was over.

And Roxie wasn't with him.

He threw the covers back, hauled his ass out of bed, and with a glance through the shadows at the bathroom, the door of which was open, he prowled out of the room.

He stopped dead one step in the kitchen when he saw her.

She was sitting on the counter, curled into herself, arms wrapped around her calves, staring out the window.

Shamus was lying on the tile of the kitchen floor right under her.

Shamus's head came up when Hank arrived, and he gave a soft woof.

That was when Roxie's head came around.

His dog's tags jingled as he loped to Hank, but Hank only gave him a distracted scratch while on the move to his woman.

He slid a hand along her waist to curl his fingers in on the other side, wrapped his other hand around her ankle, and tried real hard to get his heart from jackhammering out of his chest.

Because this was strange.

Roxie was a MacMillan. She was a Logan. Crazy came with the package.

But this was different.

"You okay?" he whispered.

"You know what's the worst?" she whispered back.

He braced.

He was a cop. He knew a lot of worsts.

What happened recently to a member of their crew was some of the worst that worst could get.

What happened to Roxie was too.

She didn't seem to have to process what Billy Flynn did to her too much. She'd had her rough patch when Vance brought her home. They'd worked through how she felt it sullied her so she wasn't good enough for him, and they fought their way to their normal.

But he'd been around shit like this his entire career. He'd heard his dad telling his mom about it while he was growing up.

He knew it could come back to bite you.

"No, sweetheart, what's the worst?"

She tipped her head to the window.

"That tree looks amazing."

He looked out the window, tightening his hold on her ankle, because it did.

Before Roxie, Hank had zero Christmas decorations. He was a single guy who spent the last thirty-five years at his parents' place for Christmas. He didn't feel the need to buy them, mostly because he knew, when he found his woman, they'd do it up like he and Roxanne did it.

Together.

They decided to go for what they needed, tree and some things around the house, and add on as the years went by. So they bought a lit wreath for the door, Hank hung it and set the timer to light it, and for this year, that was all they did outside.

That meant the huge tree in his front yard gleaming with an abundance of bright white lights in the dark against the snow shone like a cheerful Christmas beacon.

Sometimes, less was more.

"Mom was right," Roxie went on.

He wanted to smile.

He didn't smile.

He focused on her profile.

"Why are you sittin' on the countertop in the dark, Sunshine?" he prodded.

Her answer made Hank go completely still.

"Because today was the best day ever, in my whole life, and I don't want it to end."

It was Christmas night, actually probably the day after, considering what he suspected was the time.

And she was right.

It had been a great fucking day.

She turned from staring at the tree to look into his eyes.

"I love how much Mom loves holidays," she admitted. "I love her cheesy hash browns and egg casserole. I love how crazy it is with paper and ribbon and Christmas music playing. I loved how Shamus was in seventh heaven with all the mess and people. I loved watching Tex watch Mom and how happy he looked. How he looked like he'd finally come home, even though he was nowhere near Indiana, just being around Mom being Mom was home to him."

He saw the tears shimmering in her eyes, knowing what she said about Tex was as big as it could get, and having felt that same feeling watching Tex settle back into the family who'd missed him for far too long, and now had him back.

Hank used his hand around her waist to pull her into his chest.

Roxie kept talking.

"I love that Nancy and Lottie came over. I love that Tex had somewhere else to go because he's part of a huge, wide family, and went with them to Blanca's for dinner. I love that for our dinner, we sat around a big, loud, happy table at your folks' house. I love how Mom gets along so great with your mom. And Dad gets on so great with your dad. And how Ally eggs mom on. And how Indy and Lee are so much in love, and the way they show it."

"Yeah," he agreed when she paused.

"I loved that Vance sounded good when we called him. And I love the present you got me, Whisky." Her hand drifted to her neck, and she toyed with what dangled there. "This necklace is beautiful."

He didn't make a mint. So he had no choice but to get her some little things for her stocking, because the big thing was a diamond pendant.

It wasn't much, three quarters of a carat. But it hung on a platinum chain and was embedded in the bottom of a short, delicate platinum wand.

She'd lit up when she saw it, and then burst out crying, both before she threw herself in his arms and carried on about how it was too much, but how much she loved it, and it was *perfect for her*, so it was worth every penny of the money he'd gone over budget to spend on it.

She'd put it on immediately (after crying, hugging, carrying on then kissing him).

She still had it on.

"And I love that I never have to buy clothes again," he gently teased, though he didn't lie.

He had new jeans, trousers, sweaters, shirts, thermals, Henleys, not to mention underwear, socks and pajama bottoms. He was the last one opening presents, and Trish was nearly as generous as her daughter, so that was saying something.

Roxie leaned her shoulder into him. "And I loved sharing all of that with you."

At that, he drifted a hand up her spine to her neck and into her hair before he bent his head and kissed her, deep.

When he was done, she rested her head on his shoulder, and they both looked out the window.

"You like them, don't you?" she asked the window.

"Herb and Trish?"

"Yeah."

"They're impossible not to like."

She relaxed deeper into him and agreed, "Yeah."

"So you're out here, sittin' on the counter, starin' outside, because you don't want this day to end?"

She took her head from his shoulder and tipped it back to look at him. "This is a day I never want to erase."

He smiled gently at her, got close and shared, "It doesn't have to be over yet."

Her gaze heated.

Oh yeah.

He could drown in the deep blue of her eyes. He knew that the second he laid eyes on them.

Since then, he'd been sucked under, countless times. He didn't mind. It was warm in there. And the sun was always shimmering on the surface. A never-ending promise.

Perfect.

"Do I have to ask what you have in mind?" she inquired.

No. She didn't.

He moved his hand at her ankle to hook her behind her knees and lifted her off the counter.

Holding her against his chest, Roxie slid her arms around his shoulders, and Hank carried her to their bed.

Shamus followed, and Hank waited until the dog made it into the room before he kicked the door shut behind him.

But Shamus knew this drill very well, so he didn't even try to hit the bed.

He collapsed with a doggie groan on Hank's side.

Hank put his woman on the bed and then covered her with his body.

This was an occasion. One of many. Their first Christmas together.

And their first Christmas night together.

So he was going to make it memorable.

And if Roxie didn't want the day to end (even if it already had), he'd give her that too.

Therefore, he took his time. He let her take hers. It was touch and taste and sighs and moans and scratches and tickles and whispered words and soft laughter and sucking and biting and finally, grasping and panting and urgency.

And a whole fuckuva a lot of love.

After, curled close into Roxie's right side, with Shamus sprawled on her left, Hank splayed his hand on her belly and thought of what it'd look like after he planted babies there.

"I hope your worst is always having to admit your mom is right about something," he murmured in her ear.

She covered his hand on her belly. "We still have Luke, Ally, Mace and Hector to get through. Maybe Darius. I'm thinking that time won't be for a while."

It sucked, but he knew she was thinking right.

"We'll make it through," he promised.

The second these words came out of his mouth, her fingers curved tight around his, almost like a reflex.

He knew what that meant. She didn't need to say it.

He knew it. He felt it in his gut, his bones, his heart.

That was who he was. It was what he was always meant to be.

What he didn't know, until he laid eyes on Roxanne at Fortnum's the first time she walked in, was that all of it was in preparation, waiting for her.

To be her shoulder.

Her rock.

Her sounding board.

Her protector.

Her man.

It was just good to know she knew it too.

"Go to sleep, Sunshine," he urged.

"Okay, Whisky," she whispered but didn't let go of his hand.

She held it there, all night.

And their first Christmas a memory neither of them would forget, Hank woke up with her hand right there, curled around his, the next morning.

TRACK 4
ROCK CHICK RENEGADE

His

Boo

This was unacceptable.

Since the New Human showed (who Boo liked, he smelled good and Boo liked the way he looked at Boo's Primary Human), Boo's schedule had been disrupted.

Boo wasn't thrilled about this, and as was his duty, he let them know at his every convenience.

But no one, not even the human next door (who he considered his Secondary Human), had come to feed him his breakfast. (He was thinking with the way his Primary looked at the New Human, that human was going to be the new Secondary Human, and the next-door human was going to be, well...the Next-Door Human, known to other humans as "Nick").

Next-Door Human did not excel at the simple feat of breakfast. He didn't break up Boo's food like Primary did. She knew exactly how he liked his breakfast, though, her portions were puny, and he wasn't fond of the fact she didn't make up for them with his required amount of treats. She was also a good cuddler, she liked to talk to him as much as he liked to talk to her, and she kept his litter box clean. Therefore, he didn't complain...too much.

But still, unbroken-up-correctly food was better than *no food at all*.

The light outside had gone up and down, and still, *no breakfast*.

He didn't count his kibble, of which there was plenty. Everyone knew kibble didn't count.

So.

Entirely...

Unacceptable.

So unacceptable, obviously, when he heard the key in the door in the back, he jumped off his throne at the front by the window (he had many thrones, indeed, every surface in the house was his throne) and pranced toward the kitchen to let them know *precisely* how he felt about this delay.

He saw the light switch on before he got there.

He entered the room, noted it was New Secondary, not Primary (which wasn't entirely unusual, but he still found it concerning).

And then he got a good look at New Secondary's face: the human Primary called "Vance."

Boo decided to delay his litany of complaints because something really was not right.

New Secondary (that was Vance) took two steps in, his eyes never leaving Boo.

Boo didn't take his eyes off Vance either.

Then the human did something funny.

And Boo knew.

He knew.

So when Vance folded down, right on the kitchen tile, sitting cross legged, still staring at Boo, Boo knew right what to do.

He jogged to Vance, stepped right in, circled in on himself in Vance's lap, and he got to work purring.

Vance's strong fingers sifted through Boo's fur.

"She's gonna be okay," Vance whispered.

Boo had no idea what that meant, but he wasn't all fired up about the tone, so he concentrated harder on purring.

Vance kept stroking him. "She's gonna be all right."

It'd take a lot of work purring to get Vance sorted out to finally get up and get Boo some food.

He broke it up just like Primary did (known amongst the humans as "Jules").

So when Vance put it down, it was perfect.

But Boo didn't eat it.

He sat on the toilet while Vance took a shower.

He sat in the hall and watched Vance put on clothes.

And he sat in the kitchen and watched Vance leave out the back door.

He still didn't go eat.

No.

He didn't.

It would come to be his and Vance's secret. He'd have some kibble so he could keep his strength up (purring took a lot out of you, and so, he would find, did waiting).

But until she came home, he wasn't hungry.

He was in the kitty carrier in the back seat.

So, okay, they set him up in the middle so he could see a little of

them and a lot of the front of the moving machine, and that was
better than being in the seat and having nothing to look at but the
back of another seat.

And she was with them.

Finally.

It had been *forever*.

But this was intolerable.

"*Meow!*" he shared his thoughts.

She turned and looked around the seat at him.

"It's okay, Boo."

He had no clue what she was saying (other than knowing his
name was Boo), but considering she didn't end it by reaching out and
releasing him from this prison, he shouted, "*Meeeeeeeooooow!*"

"We're going to be at the cabin soon," she promised.

He didn't know what that meant either, and she *still* did not free
him from his unearned incarceration, so he told her exactly how he
felt about that.

"Meow. Meow. Meowmeowmeow. *Meow!*"

"He hates his carrier," she told Vance, who was where Boo should
be. Everyone *knew* when they were in the moving machine, Boo sat
in the lap of the person at the wheel.

How was he supposed to help if he was stuck in confinement in
the back?

"I don't know how he's gonna react to you being with us, and
you're not a hundred percent, Princess. I don't want him jumping on
you."

Boo didn't understand that either, but he knew it didn't bode
well, so he aimed his next, "*Meow!*" at Vance.

"We're gonna be there, half an hour, tops," Vance assured.

Even if he didn't know what he was saying, he still read the tone,
and Boo was far from assured.

"Meow!" Boo put in.

Jules turned to look at him, and said in his most favoritist voice,
"Love you, baby. Missed you *so much*."

Ugh.

Whatever.

Might as well use this time for some obsessive grooming so he could get a good hairball worked up and hurl it out as their punishment.

So he set about doing that.

They were back in the wilds, a domicile Boo approved of.

He liked the smell. He liked sitting in the window and lording over all the critters outside who were too foolish to know how to bend humans to their will so they gave in to your (almost) every whim. He loved that he could tell Vance was at home here and Jules was relaxed here.

Even though she was holding herself funny, he didn't love that.

But it was morning. She was still in bed.

And Vance had just put his food bowl down in the kitchen.

Boo looked at the food perfectly prepared, then up at Vance.

Vance was staring down at him.

Boo shoved his face in the food.

He didn't know what Vance said, but he felt the stroke down his spine, and heard the relief in his tone when he whispered, "That's it, cat. It's all good. Mama's home."

Boo ate and ate and licked the bowl clean when he was done.

But don't worry, he shoved some food out on the floor with his nose so they'd have to clean up after him.

He was happy Jules was back, ecstatic (though he'd be careful not to let that show overly much).

But he was never derelict in his duties.

Boo carried out his complete inspection of her the first chance he got, and it wasn't easy to find that chance. Vance was always there, helping her get around, stretched out next to her on the bed, sitting on the couch with her head in his lap while he read and she listened to music.

He was an animal. He was intuitive.

He knew his playground (her body) was not accessible at this moment, so he couldn't go gallivanting on the bed when they were both in it. There wasn't enough room.

So when Vance went to shower, Boo jumped up on the bed (and yes, he *did* mean to miss the top so he had to sink his claws into the covers and pull himself up, he had to keep his claws sharp...*obviously*), and he gave her a good once-over with his eyes and nose.

She smelled like Jules.

She smelled like home.

So he cuddled into her side and allowed her to scratch behind his ears while she babbled at him words he'd never understand.

Vance came back, and Boo had to skedaddle as he helped her up and to the bathroom.

Vance returned alone, and Boo noted it was going to be more of this lazing about they'd been doing, which Boo wholeheartedly supported.

To share this, while Jules showered, when Vance got dressed and laid back down on the bed, Boo joined him, and there were no limits to this playground, so he settled right in on his chest, shut his eyes, and the instant Vance's strong fingers started to give him a neck massage, he started purring.

"Home," Vance murmured.

Boo didn't know what that meant either.

But he knew two things.

One, it was directed at Boo.

And two, Vance really, *really* meant it.

Vance

When he pulled into Shirleen's driveway and idled, and neither of the boys moved, he knew something was up.

He turned to Roam in the front seat, who was looking around the back at Sniff.

After school, they'd come to the office and done their homework in the surveillance room, which happened a lot these days, then they'd done some surveillance in the surveillance room.

Twenty minutes ago, Shirleen texted, *If you don't have my boys home in twenty minutes, I won't be responsible for what I do.*

She was down with surveillance. She was down with the fact that Monty, or Mace, and sometimes even Luke would go over their homework to make sure they got shit right.

But they had a weekday curfew of nine o'clock, and right then, it was ten past.

"Talk to me," he ordered.

Roam's steady gaze came to him, but as usual, it was Sniff who talked.

"We want you to teach us how to drive."

Vance looked over his shoulder at Sniff. "I thought Shirleen was teaching you how to drive."

"Yeah, she is. Like a grandma," Sniff replied.

He couldn't imagine Shirleen did anything like a grandma, including drive, so this was surprising.

"She's probably just going cautious," he suggested.

Roam chimed in. "We drive every Saturday with her. Sniff for an hour and a half, me for an hour and a half. We've been doing this for six weeks. And she doesn't let us go over thirty in a forty, we haven't parked the car in a parking lot, much less parallel, and we haven't been on the highway. We just drive around for three hours, pulling up in her driveway halfway through to switch out drivers. We're real good at reversing out of the driveway and driving, and that's it. When we ask her if we can do more, she tells us we're not ready. But we are. We're real fuckin' ready."

Jesus.

She was teaching them to drive like a grandma.

And they were both turning sixteen soon, and like any teenager, they wanted the freedom of a driver's license.

"I'll talk to Shirleen."

He said that.

What he meant was, he'd talk to Jules and Jules would talk to Shirleen.

Slowly, as time went by, it was shifting (case in point, the curfew and text). But Shirleen deferred a lot to Jules. She looked to her for guidance with the boys.

It was smart. She was a childless woman who took on two runaway teenagers. And Jules had a lot of experience with runaway teenagers.

But she was finding her way, and Jules would eventually guide her into taking over.

Though now, someone had to teach them how to drive.

That was going to be him, but it was Jules who would talk to Shirleen about it.

Their relief filled the cab.

"*I'm waiting!*" Shirleen called from the open doorway to her house where she was standing.

"She's gonna go over homework Monty already went over," Roam muttered. "Even knowin' Monty went over it."

"Let her," Vance advised. "She gets something important out of it. It's no hassle for you to give it to her, so give it to her."

Roam nodded.

"You da man," Sniff said.

Vance sighed.

Sniff punched him in the shoulder and swung out. Roam held up a closed fist, Vance bumped it, then he swung out.

Vance waited until the door closed on that new family, then he reversed out of Shirleen's drive.

When he got home, Boo was waiting at the back door for him, filled with news of his day.

Vance ended the conversation by picking him up and curling him like a baby to his chest.

He then went right to Boo's treats.

Boo was snarfing them down, fingers to fangs, when Jules strolled in.

Vannce's heartrate, never quite right when he was away from her, settled.

Her gaze went from him to her cat, back to him.

"The vet said he was chonky," she reminded him.

Vance quit feeding him treats because Boo turned his pointy face her way and glowered at her.

"Cats are supposed to be chonky," he returned, which meant he got Boo's attention again, so he gave him another treat.

Jules came fully into the kitchen and rested a hip to the counter. "They're not. If they were, the vet wouldn't have pointed out he was chonky."

Vance answered that by giving Boo another treat.

"We talked about this, Crowe," Jules snapped. "We're supposed to cut down on his treats, not give him more."

He'd never told her Boo had barely eaten while she was in the hospital. And if she didn't notice her cat had lost weight, he wasn't going to point it out. She'd had her recovery to concentrate on. She didn't need to worry about her pet.

Therefore, as far as Vance was concerned, he and Boo were working on getting him back to his fighting weight.

He fed him another treat.

Boo ate it, still purring.

"I hope you don't spoil our daughter like that," Jules remarked in a way that had Vance's eyes racing to her.

What he saw on her face made him go completely still.

They'd decided. Once the doc told her it was all systems go. Once she was back to her normal self physically, they decided.

Life was too short. It was too filled with shit.

They weren't going to wait.

On any of it.

Marriage. Babies.

Everything.

They were going to do it all right away.

Therefore, she went off the Pill she'd barely got on, but they'd been told it might take a few months for her cycle to regulate.

Maybe it didn't take that long.

"What are you saying?" he asked.

"I took a test. Positive. So I went out and bought another test just in case. Positive. So I got an appointment with my OB, and she confirmed it. I'm pregnant."

Vance bent to drop Boo to his feet, scattered about fifteen treats across the floor, Boo purred a "Mrreow!" in excitement and chased after them, just as Jules cried an irate, "Crowe!"

But Vance was across the room, in her space, in her face, framing her head in his hands.

His eyes roamed her face.

She was the most beautiful woman he'd ever seen. More beautiful than anyone on a movie screen. More beautiful than any in the pages of a magazine.

And she was his.

His.

And she was having his baby.

His.

"I take it you're happy," she whispered.

He crashed his mouth down on hers and answered that question with his tongue.

When he lifted his head, she breathed, "You're happy."

"Yeah, I'm fuckin' happy," he replied.

Her violet eyes lit with joy as she returned, "Good. We're naming her Rebecca Ann."

"We're naming *him* Max."

"It's not a him, Crowe."

"It's a him, Princess."

"How can you know? I'm only six weeks. She's a mass of cells now."

"I just know."

"Whatever," she mumbled.

He took his hands from her head and slid them around her body, drawing it up against his. "Who have you told?"

"You, and only you. That's all either of us are going to tell. Even Nick and May need to stay in the dark until I reach the three-month zone."

He could be down with that.

Still, he was telling the men. Doing the cigar shit, the whole damned thing.

She watched him a beat, then her face screwed up. "You can't tell the guys."

"They won't say anything."

"They're sleeping with half the girls!" she shot back. "And they have big mouths."

"Not when it's important."

She couldn't argue that, so she didn't try.

Instead, she said, "If it's a boy, we're naming him Harry."

"No. Max. Then our next one is Sam. The one after that will be Rex."

"You have it all figured out."

"Yup."

She rolled her eyes, let that go, then asked, "Did you eat dinner?"

"Yup."

"Wanna celebrate me getting knocked up?"

He grinned at her and answered.

"Yup."

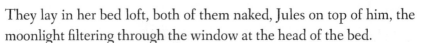

They lay in her bed loft, both of them naked, Jules on top of him, the moonlight filtering through the window at the head of the bed.

She had her face in the side of his neck, her finger drawing on his shoulder.

"You can tell the guys," she whispered. "But really, I want it on the down low with everyone else. Life has a tendency to—"

He cut her off by using his arms already around her to squeeze her tight. "Nothing's going to happen."

"I don't want everyone to get excited for us and then put them through something else after they went through all that business with what Shard did."

He tucked his chin in his neck in an attempt to see her.

"What's this?" he asked.

She lifted her head and looked down at him. "Thanksgiving in a hospital room isn't a lot of fun, Crowe."

"Maybe you were still thinking you were an angel, because if you paid attention like I paid attention, you'd have seen a bunch of people who didn't give two shits that they were celebrating Thanksgiving in a hospital room. They were just happy you were alive."

"Yeah, normally you don't make your friends have to feel happy you're alive. They just take that for granted."

"Do you think Roxie should feel guilt for being beat to shit and abducted?"

"No."

"Do you think Jet should feel shit because her dad's loan sharks focused on her to get him to pay, and some asshole was incapable of a blow to his manhood, so he wanted to make her pay?"

"No, of course not, Vance, but—"

"Listen, Princess, I'm down with you not wanting anyone to

know for a few weeks. But you're fit. You're healed. Roam's fit. Him and Sniff are in a good home, being looked after by a good woman. They're even in school. Our shit times are over." He rolled her to her back and spread his hand over her belly. "Now it's about making babies, getting married, and raising our family."

She stared up at him through the moonlight. "Are you asking me to marry you?"

"Kid's gonna have my name when he comes out every way that can be, Jules. Legally. Whatever god you pray to. All that shit. And if I'm your husband, they'll probably give me the birth certificate to fill out, so I can put in the right name."

She narrowed his eyes at him. "So you want to marry me so you'll win on the name?"

He knew she was bickering because that was what they did. It was playful and it was loving, and it was them.

But when he answered, he was dead serious.

"No. I'm gonna marry you because I love you. I'm gonna marry you because you're not only the best woman I've ever met, you're the best person. I'm gonna marry you because my heart doesn't beat right when I'm not with you. I'm gonna marry you because we're going to make beautiful babies. You're gonna be an amazing mother. And you're going to teach me how to be a good dad. I'm going to marry you because I want to spend every Thanksgiving and Christmas and birthday with you until I die. I'm going to marry you because you're *mine*. I want that legal. I want that binding. In the eyes of the law and whatever gods there are out there to pray to. So tomorrow, I'm going to get you a ring you won't ever want to take off. And as soon as we can manage it, I'm going to add a band to it. And for the rest of our days, you're at my side and in my life, Jules, as my woman, the mother of my children, and my wife."

The unshed tears in her eyes that were shining in the moonlight glimmered at him as she whispered, "Your heart doesn't beat right without me?"

"Does yours without me?"

Her whisper was even quieter when she gave him the answer he knew.

"No."

"So we doin' this?"

"Yes."

He kissed her. He did it a long time.

And when he was done, they were face-to-face, heads on the pillows, bathed in moonlight.

Boo came up and settled by draping himself across their ankles.

"You don't need me to teach you to be a good dad, Vance. You're very patient."

"We'll see."

"You are. You're great with Roam and Sniff. They love you."

They loved her. He just came with the bargain.

She cupped his cheek. "They love you, Crowe."

"Whatever you say, Princess."

She grinned at him. "And my baby pug loves you too. He thinks you're the shit."

Vance chuckled.

"Not to mention," she went on. "You've kinda stolen Boo."

"Not true," he negated. "He's all yours. He's just accepted me as an official minion."

That was when she chuckled.

She stopped doing it to say, "I want your mom at our wedding."

"I'm sure she'll be happy to come."

And he was more than sure she would.

"Something simple. Not a big deal. That's not us," she decreed.

He was totally down with that.

He'd heard of Tod's wedding planner book. He wanted no part in that shit.

"You're right. That's not us."

"Justice of the peace?" she suggested.

He grinned at her.

"Perfect."

The next morning, Jules was off to the shelter by the time Vance, with Boo tucked in his arm, moved across the back room to Nick's door.

He knocked.

Nick opened it, looking about ready to head off to face the day.

"Hey, Vance, everything good?"

"Yeah, got a second?"

Nick nodded and stepped back.

Vance and Boo walked in.

"You two have really bonded, hunh?" Nick said, smiling at Vance and his cargo.

"Until there was no pain, and she was getting around a lot better, he didn't step on her. Not once. Never had a pet, don't know if they sense that kind of shit. But yeah. He gave her the space she needed, we bonded."

Nick was still smiling, and maybe reading between the lines, though he couldn't know that the only true comfort Vance had in those early days was a clumsy, talkative black cat who curled up in his lap and kept him company in the dawn after his darkest hour.

"You had coffee?" Nick asked.

"Yep."

His eyes twinkled behind his glasses, already knowing the answer when he asked, "Breakfast?"

"I'll pick something up on the way to the office. And I know you're heading out, so I'll do this quick. I already asked her. She said yes. But I want to do this right. For both of you. For all of us."

Nick leaned back against the counter and crossed his arms on his chest, never taking his gaze from Vance. "What's up?"

"I'd like to know you're good with me and Jules getting married."

He watched Nick's body start, then he watched his eyes get wet.

Vance scratched Boo's head, giving Nick a minute.

After that minute, Nick cleared his throat and answered gruffly, "I'm honored you're gonna be an official member of the family."

Vance jerked up his chin.

"She's pregnant, isn't she?" Nick whispered.

Vance said nothing, just held his gaze.

Nick explained. "I went over the other day. Let myself in. Heard her puking in the bathroom."

His felt his spine snap straight. "Jules was puking?"

Nick's brows went up. "She hasn't told you?"

"No," Vance grunted.

"Well, I didn't either."

Vance nodded to affirm he got what Nick was saying.

"She's worried," Nick told him.

"She would be," Vance replied.

"She's also worried that you'll be worried."

Fuck.

Nick pushed from the counter, approached, clapped him on the arm then clasped him there.

"It's gonna be okay. It's gonna be amazing. She's not going to be able to hide getting sick forever. She'll settle in. It's all gonna be as it's supposed to be."

Yes. It absolutely fucking was.

"Yeah," Vance agreed.

Nick clapped him on the arm again.

Vance headed to the door, saying, "I'll let you get on with your day."

"Vance?" Nick called when he was standing in the open door.

He turned back.

Nick's voice was back to gruff when he said, "I'm so damned happy for you. For you and Jules. Damned happy."

Nick swallowed.

Then he finished.

"And Reba would be too."

"Thanks, man," Vance said quietly.

Nick nodded.

Vance and Boo went out the door.

And he took his little furry boy home.

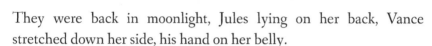

They were back in moonlight, Jules lying on her back, Vance stretched down her side, his hand on her belly.

"You gonna rest your hand on my stomach every night for the next seven and a half months?" she teased.

He looked from her belly to her. "Yes."

She stared at him.

Then she did an ab curl to touch her mouth to his before settling again.

"You got any symptoms yet?" he asked.

"Throwing up," she said without hiding or hesitation. "That's why I took the test. It's a weird kind of nausea. I've never felt anything like it before. And since we went off birth control..." She shrugged against the sheets and let that lie.

"Anything I can do?" he offered.

Her face warmed and her voice went soft. "I don't think so. But thanks."

"Talked to Lee. He's not going to give me any assignments that take me out of town throughout the pregnancy."

Her face grew surprised. "That's not necessary, Crowe."

He put gentle pressure on her belly. "I'm not missing this, Jules. Not a second of it. I'm here, for you, for him. I'll work, but I'll be close. Lee didn't blink when I asked. He's happy for us. Told me whatever I need. It's good."

"Crowe—"

He dipped down so he was nose to nose with her and enunciated each word clearly. "Not. Missing. A. Second."

She gave in a lot faster than he expected by lifting a hand and curling it around his head. "Love you, Vance Ouray Crowe."

"Love you too, Princess."

She didn't have to do an ab curl to get her kiss that time.

He gave it to her.

But as he did, he didn't take his hand from Max, growing and getting strong in the fierce protective womb of his warrior mother.

And for the next seven and a half months, his woman got used to getting it just like that.

TRACK 5
ROCK CHICK REVENGE

Hanky-Panky

Luke

Luke wasn't sure how he made it to the offices considering he was so furious he couldn't see straight.

This was why, the minute he hit reception at Nightingale Investigations, Mace came out of the door that led to the back offices.

The men of NI weren't a team.

They were brothers.

So they knew.

"Check it," Mace said low after taking one look at Luke and planting himself between Luke and the door.

Luke halted and locked eyes with Mace.

The man was right. He needed to check it.

No.

What he needed to do was go out and run—*hard*—to burn off the emotion. He'd learned that dealing with his dad while growing up. There was only so much shouting you could do. Only so much shit you could eat. When you hit your limit, you had two choices, and both were physical, but only one would allow you to sleep at night.

He didn't need to come face-to-face with the man Lee had told him was in the office and go the wrong way of physical.

He needed to check it.

He took in breath through his nose.

Mace watched him and didn't move a muscle.

He took another breath. When he let it out, Mace relaxed.

The door behind Luke opened. He twisted and watched Vance walk in.

Luke knew Lee was there as well as Mace and Monty. If they needed to lock him down, they'd have a time of it, but those men could do it.

So Vance didn't show for that.

Vance showed because he knew who was in Lee's office.

And as he'd noted, these men were his brothers.

Luke dipped his chin to Vance then turned back to Mace.

Mace opened the door for him.

Luke felt Mace and Vance at his back as he walked into Lee's office, but they didn't go in.

He knew they'd stay close, though.

When Luke entered, Lee stood from sitting behind his desk, his eyes on Luke keen, alert.

Luke spared him a glance to let him know he had it under control.

Then he turned his attention to the man sitting in a chair in front of Lee's desk.

And that control slipped.

He looked good. Tan. Healthy. Happy.

So much so, he appeared five, ten years younger than he really was.

A total turnaround from the man Luke knew fourteen years ago.

Looked like life was good for Adrian Barlow after he walked out on his family.

He watched Adrian slowly take his feet, his eyes widening as they moved up Luke from boots to face, then a broad smile spread on his face.

"Whoa. I mean, I knew you'd grow up to be something, but wow, son, just...wow," Adrian said, still smiling. "You're not something. You're something else."

It was clearly positive what that "something else" meant, but Luke had zero fucks to give a compliment from the man who'd left Ava a helpless kitten to fend for herself in a feral cat's den.

"You wanna tell me why you're here, Adrian?" he asked.

The man's smile faltered, his gaze shot to Lee, back to Luke, and he explained, "I saw a picture of you in the paper. Or, at least, a man who I thought was you. It was grainy and you were in the background. So I came to check it out, and I was right. The caption didn't have your name, but it said you were a member of the Nightingale Investigations team." He put his hands out to his sides. "So here I am."

Luke knew that picture. It had been printed after Ava was in a car that collided with a police barricade, and they got her out before the vehicle exploded.

The paper didn't print the part about Ava, so Adrian didn't know that bit.

"That explains why you thought I was here," he noted. "Not why *you* are here."

Ava's father's face lost a little color, and he opened his mouth, but Luke spoke again before he could say anything.

"Where you been Adrian?"

He asked, but he knew.

Ava said she didn't want him looking for her dad, but after

surviving five Rock Chicks, and especially what his woman went through, Luke wasn't leaving anything to chance. Ava had taken enough knocks from her family, she wasn't going to take any more. And if she had to, he was going to do what he could to soften the blow.

So he knew exactly where Adrian had been for fourteen years, and that was a part—a small part but an important part—of why Luke was so...goddamned...*pissed*.

"Luke—" Adrian began.

"Nice tan. Livin' it up while your wife tried to figure out how to finish raisin' three girls after you left?" Luke pushed.

Color started to replace the pale, and Luke wasn't sure if it was embarrassment or anger.

He had zero fucks to give to that too.

The words sounded tight when the man spoke, "You were always close to Ava."

"Yeah," Luke confirmed. "I was always close to Ava."

"So I thought maybe...you still were."

Luke didn't reply to that, but he didn't like where this was going.

He could guess this was where it was going, but he wouldn't let his mind go there because he was hanging by a thread already. He didn't need to make it snap.

Adrian took in a visible deep breath and let it out saying, "Listen, you haven't made what you feel about the decision I made all those years ago a secret—"

Luke cut in, "Nope, I made that pretty plain a few seconds ago. But I got more words on that if you want 'em."

Adrian's expression now turned hard. "No. I wanted to know if you might help me find my daughter. Ava."

Yup.

That was what he wouldn't let himself guess.

Luke felt Lee shift.

He knew why. The energy in the room changed, not in a good way, and it was all coming from Luke.

"I think I already have your answer," Adrian muttered. "So I'll be going. I can find her myself."

"You aren't fuckin' findin' her, Adrian," Luke said between his teeth, the words an unmistakable threat, and Adrian didn't miss it. Luke knew that when Adrian went completely still and stared at him. "Not interested in Marilyn and Sofia?" he asked.

"I thought I'd start with Ava."

"Strange choice, seein' as she was the one you fucked over the most."

Adrian flinched.

Oh yeah.

He knew it.

"Yeah," Luke said low.

Another threat.

So much of one, Lee murmured, "Luke."

"I got it," Luke replied to Lee without taking his eyes off Adrian.

"You don't understand what it was like in that house," Adrian shared tersely.

He understood. He understood it even before he saw Adrian for the first time in a decade and a half, looking younger than his years, fit and untroubled. Being in that house with Christine, Marilyn and Sofia had taken a physical toll on him as well as a mental one. That had been obvious. Leaving them changed his life for the better. That was obvious too.

And Luke knew all of it, the man's whole story, so he knew Adrian left the bad and found himself a whole load of good.

Still.

"I don't give a fuck what it was like."

"Luke—"

"Adrian," he leaned toward the man, "*she needed you.*" He got a lock on it and leaned back. "Not just like every girl needs her father. Ava...*needed...you.* They shredded her after you left. Tore her to pieces."

Another flinch.

Fuck this guy.

"Is she okay?" Adrian asked after he recovered.

"She's off limits to you, that's what she is."

It took some effort, but the man straightened his shoulders and declared, "She's my daughter."

"Yeah, but she's *my* woman."

The man's mouth dropped open.

Then, like he couldn't stop it, a smile bloomed on his face and a light lit in his eyes before he mumbled to himself, "I knew it. I knew you two would get together. She just had to get a little older. She loved you like crazy, and you felt the same. But big brother love turns, I see, when the flower fully blooms."

"I'm not reminiscing with you, Adrian. I'm tellin' you to go back where you came from and leave this alone."

The hard came back to his face. "That's not your decision to make."

"No. It isn't. But a coupla months ago, when I asked her if she wanted me to find you for her, she said no. So there you go."

The man blanched and some of his vim and vigor leaked out. "She said no?"

"She said no," Luke confirmed.

"Maybe, if she knows—" Adrian tried.

Luke cut him off. "Maybe if she knows you were here, talkin' to me, she'd change her mind. Maybe if she knows, after half of her lifetime you finally came lookin' for her, she might have it in her heart to hear what you have to say. And I'll tell her that, Adrian. She deserves to know. And when I tell her, I'll also tell her you've been in Castle Rock the last fourteen years. Thirty fuckin' miles away and nothing. Not a dollar to help her pay for college. Not a birthday card so she knows she's on your mind. Not...*dick*. And you were thirty...miles... *away*."

His shit was degenerating, he knew it, Lee knew it, and that was why Lee said, "Luke, brother, maybe you need to take a walk."

Luke gave his head one curt shake. "Not until he promises he'll crawl back to his rock and wait. Wait until I talk with Ava. Wait until she makes her decision." He said this to Lee, but again his eyes didn't leave Adrian. He said his next to Adrian. "You don't hear from her, you know she's excised you and that's it. You don't try to find her. You don't try to talk to her. You also don't go after Marilyn or Sofia. Ava calls this shot for all three. She deserves that privilege after you left her to them, and they've done dick to earn it back since you've been gone. But I suspect this isn't about Marilyn and Sofia. I suspect this is all about Ava."

The guilt on his face that showed clear he still didn't want anything to do with his two oldest, unless they eventually came with the package of Ava, answered that question.

That was one area where Luke didn't blame him. But he didn't share that.

He kept laying it out.

"You do hear from her, listen to me now. When she sees you, I'll be there. You dick her over again, I'll be there. But my boys who are here to make sure I got it in check will not."

"Are you threatening me?" Adrian asked.

"I'm tellin' you, you broke her heart. That's in my safekeeping now. It was then, but I fell down on the job when you left. I'm not gonna fall down again, Adrian. *That* is what I'm tellin' you."

They stared at each other.

Something bleak entered Adrian's eyes, which Luke also had zero fucks to give, and then the man said, "Fair enough."

Luke moved out of the way of the door, a nonverbal cue for Adrian to get the hell out.

Adrian took it, but he also took his life in his hands when he stopped after he came abreast of Luke.

There, he said, "You're everything he feared you'd be. So much more than he was, it ate at him. In competition to see who had the biggest balls with his own son. Everyone knew the answer to that before you even grew chest hair. Why he couldn't glory in playing a part in creating that rather than railing at it, I'll never know. I also don't know what my girl is going to decide. I deserve whatever it is. I'd like a chance to explain, but you're right. That's up to her. But I'm not leaving here without you knowing, I'm thrilled you two are together. Fate shone on you when you moved across the street from us. Not because Ava needed you. Because you needed Ava."

"Thanks for tellin' me something I already know," Luke bit out.

"And thanks for confirming you knew it," Adrian shot back.

With that, he left.

Lee gave it a beat then asked, "Want me to find something for you to throw?"

Luke angled his head from side to side, feeling the crack on the left, his shit was so tense.

Then he looked to Lee and said, "I'm good."

"You really gonna tell Ava he was here?"

"I really am. She deserves to know."

"She gonna take him back?"

"That I don't know. All I know is, I'm gonna take her back, whatever she decides."

Lee nodded.

Luke didn't.

It was quitting time.

He was headed home.

On the ride up the elevator to his loft, Luke braced.

Not because of what he had to talk to Ava about.

He always braced.

This was because he could walk into his loft, and she'd be sitting with Shirleen, watching movies that prominently featured half-naked men. She could be getting her hair done by Daisy, a do that would end up being terrifying (but he'd still fuck her with it, he knew this because it had happened). She could be half-plastered and gabbing with Sissy on the way to getting totally smashed, so he'd either have to drive Sissy home or call Dom to come and get her. She could be dabbing camo paint on her face because of some shit the Rock Chicks got themselves involved in.

It could be anything.

So bracing before was the way to go.

The doors opened up, he heard Tom Petty singing "Free Fallin'," and then his heart opened up.

Because his woman was in the kitchen, her eyes came right to him the instant he appeared, and her face split into a happy smile.

Shit, she was a knockout. So fucking gorgeous, he was constantly fighting a hard-on when he was around her.

She was also hilarious and crazy and didn't take his shit.

And Adrian wasn't wrong. Luke wouldn't be the man he became if she hadn't been across the street, looking out for him on the not-rare occasion his father got up in his face.

For starters, she taught him how to walk away rather than doing something he'd regret, something that would form him into a different man. She didn't know she did it, but she did.

She also taught him, if you give it just a little time, something good will slide in after the bad. Back then, it was her following him, coaxing him out of his shit mood and making him laugh.

Today, it was coming home to her.

"I'm cooking," she announced.

"I can smell," he said.

"No healthy living mojo tonight, honey. I scored a new client today. We're celebrating," she shared as he made his way to her.

"Fantastic," he muttered, getting smack in her space, sliding a hand from her hip to the small of her back and jerking her into his body.

When she collided, her tawny eyes fired in a way that also made him fight a hard-on, and she put her hands to his pecs.

"I should get you a club so you can drag it around and everyone will be warned of your neanderthal tendencies," she remarked.

He smiled at her.

She watched his lips do it, and she knew the score when she did that shit.

So he bent his head and took her mouth.

She was ass to the counter, he was between her legs, and her eyes were foggy just the way he liked them when he finally ended their make-out session.

"Congrats on the new client," he said.

"Thanks," she breathed.

He smiled at her again, kissed her throat then pulled her off the counter.

"What's for dinner?"

"Baked potatoes. I'm trying this new way of doing them. It's supposed to create the perfect potato. Also filet mignon. And sauteed mushrooms and haricots verts. Oh! And rolls. To finish, I grabbed some napoleons from Pasquinis for dessert."

"Jesus, with all that in my gut, I'm not gonna be able to fuck you tonight."

She shot him a look. "I've got practice with over imbibing. I'll take top."

Her saying that meant she absolutely would not. He'd find a way to rally.

She pulled out a cast-iron grill pan and put it on the stove. "Will you grill the steaks? We're almost good to go."

"You got it, baby," he murmured, turning to the steaks that were already on the counter, room temperature, salted and doused in Worcestershire sauce.

They both lived full lives, work and social.

But they had a lot of times like these.

Cooking together. Doing the dishes together. Walking down the street to Wynkoop's, hanging and sharing a couple of beers together.

They fought. This was him and Ava. Their spark never blinked out and it manifested itself in a variety of ways.

But he loved fighting with her, and not just because he loved how they made up.

There was history. There was passion. There was fire. Even in the quiet times like now, it simmered below the surface, ready to blaze however that came about between them.

He loved it. Got off on it. Fed from it.

It was going to be a good life with her. No other woman existed who could give him that. What he needed to keep his shit in line. What he needed to be the man he wanted to be. What he needed to be the man he had to be for her.

But he waited until after she loaded him down with a gut busting amount of delicious food (and whatever recipe she found did not lie, those baked potatoes were the best he'd had). After they sorted out the kitchen. But it was before she unearthed the napoleons when he guided her to the couch, sat in it, and then pulled her to straddle his lap.

"Oh boy. Looking at your face, I'm not thinking this is a lead in to hanky-panky," she noted.

His brows went up.

Christ, his woman.

"Hanky-panky?"

"Sex," she explained something he already knew.

"I know, babe. But I fuck. *We* fuck. We do not engage in hanky-panky."

"My word choice wasn't a hit to your manhood, Luke."

"You referring to it as hanky-panky, I may never get it up again," he joked.

She made a face and replied, "Oh my God. You'd turn into Lukezilla and take out half of Denver if you went even a day without getting the business."

"Correct," he confirmed, then advised. "Don't forget that."

She rolled her eyes, but her lips were tipped up.

"Babe."

She stopped rolling her eyes, and he knew she'd read his change in tone when they landed on him.

So her hands landed on him too, at both sides of his neck. "Oh

God, Luke. What's the matter?"

Total concern. It was in her face, the line of her body, the feel of her gaze, everything about her.

He gripped her hips harder where he had hold on her. Then he took one hand and slid it along the side of her neck to curl it around the back.

"I got somethin' to share."

"Okay," she whispered. "Are you okay?"

"I will be, once I tell you and I know you're okay."

Her head tipped to the side.

"Your dad showed at the offices today."

Her head righted with a snap. "What?"

"Babe—"

"He just...showed up?"

"Ava babe—"

"At your office?"

He pulled her face closer to his. "Listen to me, beautiful. Please?"

He could feel the soft pants of her breath, how her not getting enough air was making her body work, and he wished he hadn't let Mace cool him down before he confronted her father.

But now it was about his Ava.

"Breathe, baby," he coaxed.

She pulled in a shaky breath.

He waited for her to take the second one before he spoke again.

"He wants to see you."

"He wants to see me," she parroted.

"I got more you should know before you make your decision."

"Oh hell," she whispered.

"I know you told me not to look for him, but first, I didn't know if that would hold. And if you wanted it, I wanted to be in a place to give it to you. And second, I wanted to be prepared if what happened today actually happened. So I found him."

"You found him," she again parroted.

"Yeah."

"Where was he?"

He gripped her tighter and said, "Castle Rock."

It took a second, but what he expected to happen did.

She exploded off his lap.

Luke followed her up and caught her before she went ass over head over the coffee table. But once he righted her, she tore out of his hold and, skirting the coffee table, took two steps away.

He followed her.

She lifted a hand his way, stopped, and so did he.

"No, I'm okay. It's okay," she lied, and then she proved it a lie by shouting, "*Castle Rock!*"

"I'm sorry, baby," he said gently. "He's been there the whole time. Fourteen years. He's been living with a woman the last twelve." He paused, then gave it all to her. "She has two daughters. They were ten and thirteen when they met. He helped raise them."

"Oh my God," she mouthed.

And then she lost it.

He caught her before she went down and got her in bed, stretching out with her and holding her close.

She had a lot to get out, and he was glad as fuck she did it, sobbing and bucking and hiccupping in his arms. It took a long time, but eventually she wound down, sniffling, rubbing her face on his tee and burrowing into his body.

He tangled his fingers in her hair, bent his head and asked into the top of hers, "Okay?"

She nodded, but said, "I mean, not *okay* okay. Like, you know, my dad was essentially one town over, raising some other woman's kids, while we all suffered through. But I'm not going to cry or shout any more tonight." She tipped her head back to look at him and added, "Though, I reserve the right to do so at a later date. Mostly the shouting part."

He smiled at her.

She watched then shoved her face in his throat.

"What a jackass," she mumbled there.

He had a different term for it, but he didn't share.

"Hate this, baby," he said quietly. "But I'm kinda not done."

She tipped her head back again. "Do I need to fortify before this next by eating the napoleons? Special note, I referred to them in plural so I mean both of them, Luke. I'll buy you a make-up one tomorrow."

He laughed softly, fell to his back and pulled her up on his chest.

"No. You're not eatin' my napoleon. But I gotta remind you that he came lookin' for me so he could find you."

"Yeah. Unless he had some investigative work he needed done to take care of his other family, the one he stuck around to raise, and someone said my name, so with the one of you plus the one of me making two, he got curious."

"It wasn't that," Luke murmured, watching her closely.

She noticed and asked, "What?"

Luke pointed out the obvious. "He'd like to see you."

"What'd you tell him?"

"I told him I'd tell you what he wanted, and if he didn't hear from you, he needed to take that as your answer and stay out of your life. I also told him, if you went the other way, you wouldn't be seeing him without me there."

She narrowed her eyes on him. "Did you threaten him?"

She knew him down to his soul.

Therefore, he didn't hesitate to reply, "Abso-fucking-lutely."

"I kinda wish I saw that," she muttered.

He gave her a shake. "Babe."

She refocused on him and saw on his face he wanted an answer. "Do I need to decide now?"

"You can decide twenty years from now. I just wanna know you're all right."

"I'm fine, Luke."

"My tee says different. It's soaked, and I'm guessin' half that is snot."

"Ugh," she grunted.

He smiled at her.

Then he ran his fingers through the soft mass of thick hair on the side of her head and again cupped the back of her neck.

"I'm with you whatever you decide," he told her.

"What would you do?" she asked.

He shook his head on the pillow. "I know what I'd do. But I'm not you and this has to be all you."

"You wouldn't see him," she correctly guessed.

"I wouldn't waste another fuckin' second on the guy. But again, I'm not you."

Something occurred to her. It lit in her gorgeous eyes before it came out her pretty mouth, "How, exactly, did this conversation between you and Dad go? You know, aside from the threat?"

There was more than a hint of suspicion in that.

So yeah.

Down to his soul.

"We'll just say we didn't hug."

She tensed. "Oh my God, you gave him shit."

Maybe she was crazier than he thought.

"Fuck yeah, baby. He left you. He hurt you. So I didn't shake his hand and clap him on the shoulder and congratulate him on his healthy tan. I gave him shit."

Curiosity sparked. "Did he have a tan?"

"Ava babe," he began carefully. "He looked healthy. Happy. He was far from thrilled that I stood in the way of him getting to you. He was even less thrilled when I told him I'd offered to find him for you, and you declined."

Her eyes widened. "You told him that?"

"Yeah. I did," Luke affirmed. "He was happy we were together. He said he wants a chance to explain. He makes good money, lives in a nice home in an upper middleclass neighborhood with a pretty woman who loves him so much, she doesn't ask questions about why he won't marry her, seein' as he fell off her grid. Not *the* grid, but your mom's grid, so she couldn't find him, and he's still married to her. He has not suffered. He went on to better things. And regardless of what those two fuckin' sisters of yours are like, how much nagging he had to endure from your mom, he made a family and thought he had the right to just bow out. You're unhappy, you walk away. You set up a new life. You find ways to establish boundaries with your ex-partner so she won't fuck with your head. But you don't leave your children behind. Ever."

"I think I've decided," she announced.

Luke took his hand from her neck so he could wrap both arms around her tight.

"What'd you decide?" he asked.

"I've decided I'm not going to decide right now. I think it might take twenty years. Or it might take two. Or it might take until after we eat our napoleons. However long it takes, that's how long it's going to take. I'm not going to stress. I'll know when I know. Then he'll know when I know if I decide to see him. But now, I'm just going to... carry on."

Luke grinned. "That's my girl."

"You want your napoleon?"

Yup.

That was his girl.

Drama...and onward.

He flipped her to her back. "Gotta work for it."

Her gaze heated and her words were breathy when she declared, "I get top."

"You're gonna get somethin', but it isn't top."

"I thought men liked women riding them."

"I want you in the saddle, baby, I'll put you there. I'm in the saddle tonight."

She gave a side eye to nothing, muttering, "Whatever."

"Babe?"

She looked to him.

"Kiss me."

Hungry joined the heat in her gaze.

And then she kissed him.

Luke woke when the nagging pain he felt in his gut meant it was time to turn, and Ava didn't turn them.

Which meant he woke to an empty bed.

He didn't have to search for her. He knew where she was.

So he threw back the covers, padded through the loft and went to her.

He settled on the floor behind her and surrounded her with his bent legs, pulling her—curled thighs to tits, his tee stretched over her knees—into his chest.

"I should have landed a fist in his face," he growled into her ear.

She turned her head to face him. "Why?"

"You can't sleep."

"I can't sleep because I'm happy."

Luke's head jerked.

Ava kept talking.

"You were the first boy I loved. You're the only man I've loved. I have no idea what Dad showing would have done to me a couple of months ago, when you weren't in my life. And okay, I didn't handle it with smooth decorum when you told me. But...whatever. In the end, I know the blow was softer because you delivered it, and you were there to hold me while I dealt. I also know you'll support whatever I decide whenever I make the decision." She twisted in his arms and used her hands to cup his jaw. "I'm not sleeping, Luke, because I kinda don't care about Dad coming back. I've got everything I need because I've got you. And after feeling his abandonment for half my life like a hole that's never filled, and now it's just gone, that's a lot for a girl to deal with, and it isn't conducive to sleep."

Luke was dealing with a lot too.

And he had one particular way he worked that kind of feeling out when it was about Ava.

So she was on her back and he was on top of her in half a second.

"I want you to fuck me, honey, but I'm not sure about doing the business on hardwood," she whispered.

So he was up, she was tossed over his shoulder, and he stalked to the bed.

He threw her down on it, caught her ankles, flipped her to her belly, then jacked her toward him and up to her knees at the edge of the bed.

"Luke," she breathed.

He yanked her panties to her thighs.

"Luke!"

He slid his fingers through her wet.

Soaked. Always. For him.

He shoved his shorts over his ass and drilled in.

Her head flew back.

"Yes," she whispered.

Oh yes.

He fucked her in a way she'd never call it hanky-panky again.

And after, once he'd cleaned her up, repositioned her panties, and had her held close to him under the covers in their bed, was when he spoke.

"You were the first girl I loved and the only woman I've ever loved, Ava. Know it. And don't forget it."

"I won't, baby. I think you just drilled that in so deep, me forgetting that would be impossible."

"Good," he grunted. "Go to sleep."

"So bossy."

"As if you don't like it," he muttered.

She pushed closer. "Oh, I like it. *All* of it."

Fuck.

His woman.

His Ava.

He held her tight, and finally she shut up and fell asleep.

Which meant so did he.

TRACK 6
ROCK CHICK RECKONING

Just in Case

Mace

Mace returned from his run, wandering through the lush foliage that led to the bungalow he shared with Stella at the Chateau Marmont.

The band had a day off from the studio.

This was because they were on fire. Dixon Jones and the swinging dicks at Black Fat Records were beside themselves. The tracks were great, and Stella and the boys were laying them down like pros.

Mace had to admit to feeling shock about this. He thought there'd be antics. Tantrums. Fights. Groupies hanging out in the booth, distracting the process.

But there had been none of that shit.

He looked right, where the path opened up to head down to the pool, and he stopped dead.

Pong, his body glistening with oil, a tiny neon-green Speedo covering his narrow ass, a thin gold chain winking in the sun around his waist, was lying flat out on his stomach on a lounger, arms dangling down the sides to rest on the pool deck.

He looked passed out.

This could have something to do with the two women on the loungers on either side of him, one laying on her back in a barely-there bikini, the other on her stomach, no top to speak of and a thong hiked up her ass, both also looking passed out.

The Gypsies were a no-name band here in LA, and they'd only been in town for three weeks. Most of that time, they'd been working. They hadn't even played a gig.

Still, Pong scored himself some groupies.

Mace felt his lips twitch as he continued moving toward the bungalow.

He let himself in and saw Stella and a mug of coffee at the table by the back window.

Her shining, thick, long, wild hair was sexy messy, her beautiful face still held a residue of sleep.

Her gaze came direct to him. It took in his body slicked with sweat, and a hungry look pushed out the sleep on her face.

He took that hungry as an invitation.

And he accepted.

"Get in our bed," he growled.

Her eyes shot from the tee plastered to his chest, up to his face, then she got off her sweet ass and hightailed it to bed.

Sprawled across the white sheets, Mace watched Stella come out of the bathroom after cleaning up.

She stopped long enough to pull on some baby-blue panties and a tight white tank that didn't quite meet the waistband of the underwear before she put a knee to the bed and crawled into it to collapse half down his side, half on the bed.

Mace shoved a hand under her, curled it up and rested it on her ass.

She stacked her hands on his chest and took one of what had become many surveys of his face during their time in Los Angeles.

"I'm fine," he murmured, giving her ass a squeeze.

He could answer her unspoken question because he knew what was on her mind.

Tiny had lived in LA, and Mace had spent a lot of time in LA when she did.

She also died in LA.

Stella knew all this, and his woman was worried it was going to get to him.

She was right to worry.

It was getting to him.

Then again, he'd never get over losing Tiny. He just needed to fight his way to understanding that it was natural, an honor to her memory, what she deserved, and maybe that would help him live with it.

Having his mom and Chloe back was a balm he didn't know he needed.

But Stella did.

On that thought, he gave her ass another squeeze.

"You should go surfing while we're here," she suggested.

"Babe," he warned.

"I'm assuming you got so good at it because you liked to do it. Don't you miss it?"

He did.

But that held memories of Caitlin too.

He still snowboarded, and Caitlin loved her big brother, she'd been with him when he was on a mountain.

"I board," he said, not meaning to do it, not used to sharing.

It just came out.

"What?" she asked softly, her throaty voice wrapping around the word, making it feel like a soothing touch.

And another invitation.

An invitation to share more in the safe space it seemed only Stella could give him.

"I snowboard. I don't surf." He shifted on the bed, discomfort gathering in his muscles. "She came to a lot of my surfing competitions. She also came to my boarding competitions. So why do I board and not surf?"

"Do you board by yourself?"

He shook his head. "No. Sometimes Eddie comes with me, or Lee, Hank or Monty."

"So, you made it part of your new life, without her."

He had. And he did it with men he respected, living a life doing work he was proud of after all he'd done when they lost Tiny.

He couldn't say he was proud of what he'd done for Tiny.

He could only say it was a job that needed to be done, so he did it.

But what he did now with Lee and the men, he felt pride in that. In their brotherhood. In the family they gave him.

He ran the knuckles of his free hand along her cheekbone, murmuring, "You're gorgeous *and* smart."

"There's a lot to me. I'm not just a wannabe Rock God," she joked.

"Soon-to-be," he corrected.

Her brown eyes melted, and she whispered, "Soon-to-be."

"Glad we got that straight."

She pushed up so she was closer to his face, and he had her tits to his chest, not her hands. It was by a slim margin, he liked anything of her touching him, but he preferred the tits.

"Is it just me, or is it a little freaky how good the boys are being?" she asked.

"It's hella freaky," he concurred. "But when you're one album contract away from everything you ever wanted, you get your shit sharp."

She nodded.

"Though, Pong's right now passed out, flanked by two women down by the pool."

She started laughing, the husky sound taking a firm grip on his dick.

So he rolled her.

"What are we gonna do on your day off?" he asked when he had her on her back and his hands were moving on her body.

"I have a feeling you have some ideas."

Oh yeah.

He had ideas.

"Yeah," he confirmed.

She arched into him, her fingers playing the skin on his back with the same talent she played her guitar. "Let's roll with those."

He put his mouth to hers, not releasing his hold on her gaze, and said, "Perfect."

Stella was asleep.

Mace was awake.

It was late, but LA was a lot like Vegas, with a hazier, more laid-back feel. It never shut down. You could feel the vibe of the city pulsing softly over the grounds of the Chateau into their room.

Denver was a city at the same time it was a town. It got quiet at night. Shit happened and people were out doing their thing, good or bad, at all hours.

But it wasn't like LA.

And as he lay in bed on his back, Stella cuddled beside him, her head on his shoulder, her hand on his chest, it occurred to him that he'd forgotten how much he liked it.

He missed it.

He put his hand on hers at his chest and immediately felt Tiny's ring on her pinkie.

He closed his eyes to concentrate on fighting the constriction that tightened his throat.

He needed a drink.

He lifted his head to kiss the top of hers, then carefully slid out from under her, making sure the covers stayed put around her body.

He pulled on some jeans, a tee, his running shoes, and headed out.

He went straight to the bar, and he was both surprised and unsurprised to see Hugo sitting on a stool, a snifter of cognac in front of him, his gaze to Mace like he was expecting him.

Mace took the stool next to him, ordered a bourbon neat and turned to Hugo.

"Feels like you've been waiting on me, man," he noted.

"I have, and you took your time. Every night, been sitting here, expecting you to show," Hugo replied.

Mace leveled his gaze on Hugo, who, like the rest of the band (save Floyd), could do stupid shit, but even so, he was less prone to it.

If Mace had to call it, he'd say Hugo would give it five to seven years to get the wild out. Then he'd find a good woman, start making babies, and become the band's new Floyd, working with Stella to keep their shit tight and their train—which had more than enough power, it never had to meet its final destination—on the rails.

"You know what you gotta do," Hugo said.

The bartender put his glass in front of Mace. He picked it up and threw back a healthy shot before setting it back to the bar, his fingers still wrapped around.

He kept his gaze on the back of the bar.

"Take her with you," Hugo encouraged. "First, she needs to go. She needs to be there with you when you go. But she also needs that connection. And second, it's always gonna kill, but with her there, it'll lessen the pain."

He knew exactly what Hugo was talking about. What he didn't know was how Hugo knew to talk about it.

Maybe Stella had shared with him. Maybe Floyd had a conversation with him.

But Mace reckoned this was all Hugo.

"I don't know if I can," he admitted to the bottles of liquor behind the bar.

"You can. You need to. The concept of closure is bullshit. There are some wounds that never heal. This is one of them."

Mace turned his head to Hugo.

Hugo kept talking.

"But this is the journey, Mace. You can't avoid stops on the journey. You do, they'll haunt you. You got enough haunting you, brother. Don't you think?"

Mace lifted the glass and downed the rest of the bourbon.

He then jerked up his chin to the bartender for a refill.

The bartender complied.

Through this, Mace nor Hugo said anything.

Only after Mace took his next sip did Hugo speak.

"She's there all alone, brother."

Mace felt those words twist in his gut, and that feeling made him send a murderous look to the man at his side.

"She's not there."

Hugo shook his head. "She's there, Mace. And she's wondering why her brother hasn't visited her."

Mace dropped his head, clipping, "*Fuck.*"

Hugo downed his cognac, clapped him on the back and slid off his stool.

"I'll leave you with that, man, 'cause I know you'll do the right thing..." His pause was meaningful, then he landed his last velvet blow, "For your sister."

He felt Hugo's hand on his shoulder. There was a firm squeeze, then the man was gone, leaving Mace with his bourbon and his memories.

When he got back to their bungalow, Stella was again at the table. No coffee this time and sitting in the dark.

"Did you talk to him?" he asked after he shut the door behind him.

"No," she answered. "Which one was it?"

There it was.

She didn't talk to Hugo. She didn't talk to any of them.

"Floyd?" she went on, her tone knowing, love threading through it, Floyd being the only real dad she'd ever had.

"Hugo."

He could sense her surprise.

Mace moved to the couch and folded into it.

She came to him and climbed on to sit astride his lap.

She said no words. She just rested her chest to his, shoved her forehead in his neck and pushed her hands in at his back so she was holding him.

Mace didn't touch her.

"Do you believe in life after death?" he asked.

He felt her body tense, knowing she worried about giving him the wrong answer, prodding that wound that would never heal, causing him pain.

Mace knew she forced herself to relax when she replied, "I haven't landed on my decision on that, but I'd like to think yes."

"I think it's no," he shared. "I think once you quit breathing, that's the end. And when the last person who remembers you dies, that's when you cease to exist."

Stella was on him, all around him, her scent, her weight.

But somehow, she made it more, wrapping him up, holding him closer, with more than just the tightening of her arms.

Mace drew in breath, drawing her in, the strength of her love was all he ever needed.

Maybe that was it. Maybe that was why he fucked them up the first time.

Maybe he wasn't ready for Stella to give him the strength.

But now, he reminded himself, he was ready.

She'd given him the strength.

"But just in case," he whispered.

"Yes," she whispered back. "Just in case."

Mace held the huge bouquet of roses.

Stella held Mace.

When they arrived at the destination Mace had avoided until that moment with everything that was him, he saw Chloe had done well. The stone was perfect. Not huge and ostentatious, not small and unnoticeable.

A pair of ballet shoes was etched in the top. Words and numbers he refused to look at in the middle.

And at the bottom, it said, Loved by her mother and her brother and everyone who knew her.

Mace read those words.

Then he read them again.

And again.

Stella squeezed his hand.

He swallowed, let her go and crouched, putting the pink flowers at the base of the marble gravestone.

He wanted to say something, he just didn't know what to say.

Or how to say everything he had to say.

It was on this thought, he heard the guitar.

Startled, he looked over his shoulder.

He thought it was just him and Stella.

But under a tree a few rows away, stood Floyd, Hugo, Leo and Pong.

And a little nearer, Buzz and his guitar.

From the chords Buzz was playing, Mace knew what was coming, but he turned back to the flowers when Buzz started singing "Good Riddance."

Stella got to her knees behind him. He felt her hands on his lats, her forehead rest against the base of his neck.

And as Buzz sang, finally, he lifted his eyes to the words under the ballet shoes.

CAITLIN TALLULAH MASON
"TINY"

Buzz stopped singing.

The guitar stopped playing.

The song was over.

It took some time.

Then Mace knew what he had to say.

"For what it's worth, it's worth all the while."

He heard his woman's soft sob.

And after hearing that, silently, Kai Mason finally said goodbye to his baby sister.

After the gig was over, Mace moved into the dressing room, and since he'd had some practice, he clocked them immediately.

He prowled right there.

"ID," he grunted to one of the three girls draped on Pong.

"Dude," Pong started. "They been carded."

"Ohmigod, are you Kai Mason?" the girl breathed.

He snapped his fingers. "ID."

She tore her gaze from him, looked to Pong, then looked to the security guard at the door.

"Not gonna ask again," Mace warned.

Hesitantly, she grabbed the little bag that was resting on her hip from the straps that crossed her body, and she pulled out her ID.

He took it, barely glanced at it and knew it was fake.

He kept hold on it and asked, "How old are you?"

She'd practiced this, so she immediately told him the age from the ID. "Twenty-two."

"How old are you?" he repeated.

She stared at him. Then said, "Okay, nineteen."

"How. Old. Are. *You?*" he said menacingly.

She pushed away from Pong and threw up her hands. "Seventeen! Okay? But I'm almost eighteen!"

"Fuck," Pong mumbled.

"Out," Mace said to the girl.

"But—" she started.

"Out. Now," Mace ordered. Then looked to the other two girls. "You go with her."

"But I'm actually eighteen," one of them said.

"Take it up with her." He jerked his head at the one he carded. "She got you ousted. Go." When none of them moved, he warned, "I won't say it again."

The three of them studied him, wondering how far they could push it, considering they were all young, very pretty, and probably because of both, got their way a lot.

Thankfully, they were also smart because they got their asses in gear and took off.

But not before the first one requested, "Can I have my ID back?"

"Nope," was Mace's answer.

When they were gone, he went to the security guard at the door.

"I think I remember telling you to card every female that came in here, no matter what age they look," he remarked.

"I did," he returned, surly and combative.

Black Fat could put on a helluva tour.

But their choice in security sucked.

He held up the ID with two fingers a couple of inches from the guy's face. "Can you not tell real from fake?"

"It's a rock band, man. They don't care real or fake, just as long as the date is right."

"This band does."

"No, *you* do," he shot back. "Bet Pong won't be happy you kicked out the pussy he tagged as his for the night."

Mace looked over his shoulder seeing what he knew he'd see.

Pong was still lounged in the armchair as he was before, but now three other women were there, and they were all clearly of age.

He turned back to the guard and lifted a brow.

The guy's lip curled. "Dude, I know you're a shit-hot PI. And I know you're bangin' Stella. But bottom line, you're just a rock star's boyfriend."

Mace stood very still.

"Fired," Stella sing-songed as she walked in.

Stella was always late to the dressing room at the end of a gig. That's because she gave time to young women who were studying music and entered local competitions for the privilege.

Floyd gave that time with her.

The rest of the band, considering the girls were always minors, headed straight to the dressing room.

She stopped to reach up and kiss Mace's jaw. She gave him a smile.

Then she ignored the security guy and strutted into the dressing room, right to the vat filled with bottles of Fat Tire.

"Think Stella stated the case," Floyd, now standing close to Mace, added. "You're fired, bud. Get outta here."

"Pain in the ass diva bullshit," the guy groused, locking eyes with Mace. "No skin off my nose."

"Before I take the skin of your entire face, motherfucker, get the fuck out," Hugo called. "Jesus, where do they find these guys?" he asked the room at large. "It's like amateur hour."

The security guard's face got red.

Mace got close.

The man's head jerked, he finally took in Mace's vibe, and that was when he also finally got smart.

He took off.

Mace caught the door before it closed on him and looked at the two guys outside. "You let anyone in here who isn't legal again, you won't get another assignment. Anywhere. Except maybe at a mall. Am I heard?"

"Right," one grunted.

"Yup," the other one also grunted.

Clearly, those two were less dumb, or maybe they were just less assholes.

He went back to the room, letting the door close behind him.

Stella was there, handing him an open beer.

"You were the shit out there tonight, baby," he told her.

"You always say that," she replied before she put the bottle to her lips and took a tug.

"I never lie."

She blasted him with a smile, it was lit with the afterglow of a great gig, which was also a promise of off-the-hook sex when they got back to the hotel room. She did this before she strutted to the couch and threw herself on it for a much-needed rest. As always, she put everything into the show. So much, Mace was wondering how she was still conscious, much less how she'd pull out even more when she did what he knew she was going to do in about an hour, that being fucking him stupid.

She was beside Leo, who had a gurgling bong to his mouth, taking a hit.

He felt Floyd at his side.

"They'd demand people sort through the M&Ms for us if we asked," Floyd started. "They go all out. Red carpet. Five star. Top of the line. But their security is for shit. Our rise has been stratospheric, as you know, but I think you and I both also know, it's only just beginning. So the bigger she gets, *they* get, the worse that particular problem is gonna get. They don't tighten their safety procedures and the people who enforce them, I don't see good things."

This was Mace's same thought.

"You have a word?" Mace asked.

Floyd nodded.

"Three times," Floyd answered.

"Right, then I'll have a word."

Floyd smiled.

A knock came at the door and Mace twisted that way.

One of the guards had his head stuck in.

He looked right at Mace and said, "Guests." Then he jutted his chin, an indication the band would be okay with who was on the other side of the door.

Mace returned the gesture.

The door opened, and the hip-hop megastar Dee-Amond strolled in, followed by a more than impressive entourage.

"Damn, my motherfuckers," he said by way of greeting. "I heard you were planting new roots in rock 'n' roll, but hell if they didn't get that shit right."

"Holy fuck," Leo breathed, pot smoke still drifting out of his mouth, bleary eyes glued to Dee-Amond.

Hugo smiled slow.

Buzz stared.

Pong was buried in women and wasn't paying attention to anything else.

It was Stella who stood from the couch and made the approach, hand out.

"Dee-Amond, wow. Honored," she said as he took her hand.

"Couldn't believe it'd be true, you being more beautiful up close and personal, but here it is. And that voice. Damn, sis, platinum-plated."

Stella smiled at him, and the richest, most famous recording artist of the day was instantly charmed for a lifetime.

Mace grinned.

Yeah.

That was his girl.

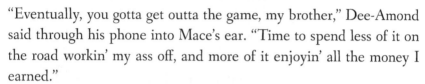

"Eventually, you gotta get outta the game, my brother," Dee-Amond said through his phone into Mace's ear. "Time to spend less of it on the road workin' my ass off, and more of it enjoyin' all the money I earned."

"I hear you," Mace replied.

"Still gonna need you, Mace. Just because I'm slowing down doesn't mean crazy motherfuckers don't want a piece of my ass," Amond went on.

"You need my services, you got 'em. You don't, you're still invited over this weekend. I'm grilling. My mom is in town."

"Lana? Is Tom with her?"

"'Course."

"Chloe and Ben coming?"

"Absolutely."

"Count me in. Have your girl talk to my girl about times and shit."

His "girl" was the woman who ran MTS Security for him so he didn't have to be behind a desk all the fucking time.

She was also sixty-seven years old and had been the executive secretary to two studio heads. Both of whom she hated. Both of whom she'd wrung top salary out of, including "retirement" packages (even when she left one at age forty-three) that meant she didn't have to work again, even in LA.

He suspected it was more about the dirt she knew about them, but she'd endure torture before she'd ever tell.

Another reason why she worked for Mace.

After her second retirement, she realized she'd become used to the excitement of the business and couldn't stay away.

Now she kept Mace's ass in gear, and all his men...and women.

"I'll get on that," he told Amond.

"Right. Later, brother."

"Later, Amond."

He'd barely put his phone down before the screen lit up with a picture of him with his seven-year-old daughter wrapped around his back, Stella pressed to his side, smiling up at Tallulah, who was smiling down at her mom. His wife's hand was on his abs.

It was only Mace who was smiling at the camera.

For a second, the past came rushing back, and he didn't know who the man in that picture was.

But he grabbed the phone, took the call from his wife, and after he said, "Hey, baby," and she replied, "Hey, Kai," he remembered.

That man was him.

Son to Lana Mason.

Stepson to Chloe Mason.

Husband to Stella Gunn.

Father to Tallulah India Jet Mason.

And...yeah. Brother to Caitlin Mason.

"What's up?" he asked.

"First, Tex and Nancy are joining us this weekend. She mentioned she'd never been to Universal Studios, so obviously Tex made it his mission to get her here. They arrive tomorrow."

"Not a problem. We got room."

And they did. They had a seven-bedroom, nine-thousand square foot house on a compound located on the north side of Malibu that included a detached studio, a casita, a pool house (so also obviously a pool) and extensive gardens.

"Second, you need to call the head of security at Universal Studios and warn them Tex is coming."

He chuckled and lied, "I'll get right on that."

He heard her husky laughter, felt it in his chest and parts south, then she said, "Tally been going on again about how she just *can't live* without Sophia."

Mace blew out a sigh.

He liked their house with its proximity to the beach, so he and Tally could surf.

Tally liked that, and the pool.

Stella liked the studio.

But all of them were done with LA.

Tally's best friend had moved to Phoenix. Now, Tally was in fits of despair—near-tween-girl style—that her bestest bestie since *forever* had left because her dad got transferred, and they weren't going to get to see each other at school every day.

He and Stella tried not to spoil their girl.

But seriously. Droughts. Mud slides. Earthquakes. Daily run-ins with fruits, nuts and flakes (no judgement, Mace was a fan of letting it all hang out and being who you were, but Mace couldn't deny he missed the solidity of Denver, there were fruits nuts and flakes there too, but not at every turn).

And living in a town where you could walk into any store, coffee shop or restaurant and see anyone from the A-list to the C-list (Stella being A-list) and have to deal with the fans who didn't have a problem asking for a selfie, or who did and took pictures of you while you were eating eggs benedict at brunch, was getting really old.

Phoenix had zero natural disasters, three-hundred-sixty-five days of sunshine, and a plot of land they'd bought in Paradise Valley, which they already had the permits to build on.

"Family meet tonight?" he asked.

"Family meet," she agreed.

"Got some things to wrap up. Should be home in a couple of hours."

"See you when you get here. I'm cooking."

Of course she was. Rock star who'd repeatedly made the cover of *Rolling Stone*, cooked for her family every night when she was home.

"Look forward to it, whatever it is."

"Okay. Later, babe."

"Later, Kitten."

He ended the call and stared at the phone.

He then swiveled in his chair and looked left to right, taking in the overabundance of framed photos on his credenza his wife and daughter added to regularly.

Mace in jeans and a white linen shirt, Stella in a white bikini that had lace applique around the hips and on the top, just under where the straps started. She was wearing a sheer duster with more lace dotted on it that fell to her thighs in the back. A single strand of flowers crowned her loose hair, and she had a long string of fresh-water pearls hanging on her neck, the end of which was an oblong peridot.

They were on a beach in Hawaii. It was their wedding.

A shot of Mace and Stella and the whole crew in the back room at My Brother's Bar. Everyone was smiling, though Tex looked like he'd just completed a murder spree.

Mace leaning over Stella who was on her back in a hospital bed, tendrils of her hair plastered to her face, her cheeks red with the effort she'd just expended, a gunked-up bundle resting on her chest with a scrunched-up face and dark hair on her head.

Chole and Ben, his mom and Tom, and Tally and Stella in front of the Christmas tree.

Tally and Mace at the foot of a run in Aspen, boards under their arms, goggles up on their helmets, smiling at the camera because Stella was behind it.

Stella and the girls in their bridesmaid dresses at Luke and Ava's wedding, Jet's large baby bump proudly displayed.

Stella and her guitar onstage at the Rock & Roll Hall of Fame when BMG did the tribute at the induction of the Pissed-Off Hippies.

Mace and Stella on the way into the Grammy's, Stella in a slim, white tuxedo with a shimmery pink top that dipped way low, Mace in a black tuxedo, white shirt, collar open. Pong, wearing more makeup and having more hairspray in his hair than Stella, was photo-bombing them.

Lee and Tally on the beach when Tally was five. She was

pointing at something in the ocean, Lee was crouched by her, one hand to her back, his head turned, looking in that direction.

And in the middle, next to their wedding picture, not hidden, pride of place, was a photo of Caitlin on stage wearing a pink leotard and matching sheer skirt tied at her waist and drifting to her knees. She was up on point, caught in motion.

Her arms were above her head, her beautiful hands held with natural grace and delicacy.

Mace looked from that picture to the one of Lee and Tally on the beach, to Stella's beaming smile in her bridesmaid dress, to the photo of them caught up in good times at Brother's. Good times that happened for no reason, just because they'd all found their family and they were smart enough to appreciate it.

Then he went back to Tiny.

"Hope I did you proud, sweetheart," he whispered, drew in breath and turned back to his desk.

As he sorted shit to get ready to go home, it didn't take long for him to finish making up his mind about a thought he'd had a while ago.

So he re-engaged his phone, went to contacts and found Lee.

"Hey, brother," Lee answered.

"Yo, Lee. Got a second to talk something through?"

There was a beat of silence and then, before Mace could lay out the plan, he knew Lee knew what he was about when he said, "Christ, man, I thought you'd never ask."

Mace felt a smile spread on his face.

Then he sat back in the chair in his office and hammered out a deal with his friend.

TRACK 7
ROCK CHICK REGRET

One One

Hector

Hector sat next to Sadie at the table in the visitation room.

Seth sat opposite them.

Sadie had her head bent and she was talking a mile a minute while sliding photos across the table toward her father.

"Her name is Gretl. She's everything. Hector gave her to me for Christmas."

Seth spared Hector a quick glance, then looked to the photo and murmured, "Adorable."

"She totally is!" Sadie gushed. "I'm going to be sad when her ears stop being floppy, but she's such a good girl. Hector got her for my protection, but she's so friendly. I'm not sure she'll be good at protection, unless the bad guy is allergic to dogs or being licked to death."

The glance Seth gave him that time lasted longer, but not too long, Sadie was sliding another photo across the table.

"That's me with the girls at Roxie's wedding. Roxie is obviously the bride." She pointed the rest out. "That's Indy, and that's Ally. There's Ava. And there's Stella. And Jet and Jules. And that's Annette, she's a hoot! And Daisy, you know. Also, Shirleen."

"That's a large wedding party," Seth noted.

"I know! Isn't it *aces*?" She asked a question, but she didn't wait for an answer. She slid another photo to him. "That's Tex. He's crazy. And very loud. But he's a total sweetheart and he makes *the best* coffee."

Seth frowned down at the picture that showed Sadie glued to Tex's side at Roxie's wedding, his arm around her shoulders crushing her there.

He was smiling at the camera.

If you were trying to be kind, you'd describe the smile as awkward. If you were telling it like it was, you'd describe it differently.

"He looks like a serial killer," Seth said.

Yup.

That's how you'd describe it.

Sadie dissolved in peals of laughter, laughter that Hector paid very close attention to in order to assess if it was fake, stressed, forced or other.

But it was real.

What unnerved him was, when he returned his attention to Seth, he knew with her father's sharp attention on his daughter, he was making the same assessment.

When she quit laughing, she assured, "He really is a sweetheart."

"I'll take your word for it," Seth drawled.

Sadie smiled at him.

And fuck him, Seth Townsend transformed when the man smiled back.

Because that was genuine too.

The bell rang, and that meant time was up.

Seth beat back his look of disappointment in record time (something else that shocked the shit out of Hector, the fact he'd let it show at all).

He then leveled his eyes on Sadie and said, "I'm glad you came, darling. I loved looking at your pictures. And please tell your friend, Jet, I appreciate the cookies. But if you don't mind, I'd like a quick word with Hector."

She paled a bit, looked between Hector and her dad, and settled on her dad.

"I do mind, Dad."

"It's not going to be bad," Seth told her.

"Then why can't you talk about it with me here?" she pushed.

Seth looked slightly sick when he replied, "Because it's up to Hector if he wants to share with you what we talk about."

"It's okay, *mamita*," he said quietly.

Sadie gave her dad a hard look before she hit Hector with the same thing.

Then she got up and warned them both, "Be nice."

She reached and grabbed her pictures, smiled at her dad, then walked around the table and gave him a quick peck on his cheek. She did this before she shot an adorable warning look to Hector, and both men watched as she walked away.

When she was out of earshot, Seth clipped. "A puppy?"

Hector turned his attention to Seth. "She loves animals."

"That's hardly enough protection, Chavez," Seth retorted. "And it'll take at least a year to train it to do what it should be doing."

"Then it's good Vance Crowe installed a security system in my place that's so much better than the one you had at your house, it's laughable. And yours was top of the line. And that Sadie agreed to keep the tracker on her car and continue to carry one in her bag. Also, to have her location monitored through her phone."

Seth puffed up his chest and huffed out a breath, which was the only way he'd share that he found that acceptable.

But Hector wasn't feeling good about this.

"There a reason I need to keep her covered?"

"No. Except she's my daughter and the worst happened to her, so I would hope you'd stay on target."

"Since that's always on both of our minds when it comes to Sadie's safety, maybe don't waste what little time we got left, and instead, ask me what you really wanna ask me," Hector ordered.

Their eyes clashed.

Then, through clenched teeth, Seth asked, "How is she coping?"

He meant about the rape, because, yeah, that was always on both their minds when it came to Sadie's safety.

It sucked the man was all in to be a good dad. It was a whole lot easier when he was a cold, heartless asshole.

"She's fine," he gritted in return. "She has good friends, two of whom know what she's been through, two others got her into counselling. She likes her counsellor. Trusts her and connects with her when needed. My mom's teaching her how to cook. She goes in next week to get fitted for another bridesmaid dress, this time, for Ava's wedding. And if we don't kill each other fighting over paint colors and shit, I'll be putting a ring on her finger soon, so she'll be getting fitted for another type of dress."

Seth's face turned to stone.

"You know it's going to happen," Hector warned low.

"There's movement on my appeal," Seth forced out.

Their case had been tight, so he muttered, "Good luck with that."

"We're appealing the sentencing, not the verdict."

Hector sat still and studied him.

"Seems the judge may have acted improperly."

"Fucking shit," Hector muttered.

He'd been concerned about this.

"You want your future fiancée's father incarcerated?"

"I want a criminal to pay for his crimes. After that's over, I'll worry about you being my father-in-law."

"Well, you'll get that. Both, it would seem. It's simply that the maximum should have been five years, not fifteen. So I'll be eligible for parole next year."

"And you didn't want to tell Sadie this because...?" Hector prompted.

Again, he looked sick when he said, "Because I don't know whether she'll be glad to hear it, or won't want to know until it happens, so she can figure out how she feels then. And you *do* know where she stands on that."

He suspected he looked sick when he replied, "She'll want to know."

Seth smiled slow. "Then you have good news to give her."

Even if Seth wasn't done, they were done.

Hector stood.

Seth waylaid him by calling his name.

He looked down at the man, and surprisingly, Seth didn't move, even if he wasn't at an equal or advantageous position.

Uncharacteristic.

"Is she giving Lizzie her gardenias?"

"Every Sunday," Hector informed him.

Seth nodded.

Right. Now they were done.

Hector weaved his way through the tables of family and friends saying good-bye to inmates to get to Sadie.

When he got to her, she didn't delay. "What was that about?"

"In the truck, *preciosa*."

She rolled her eyes.

He slung an arm around her shoulders and guided her to his truck.

When they were in his new vehicle, the one she gave him for Christmas, the heater blasting to force out the cold (and it didn't take ten minutes for the heater to do this, like it did in his Bronco), and they were on their way home, she snapped impatiently, "*Well?*"

"I see I got Attitude Sadie," he teased.

"Oh my God. This is the worst. We're close to a prison when I need to murder someone."

He burst out laughing.

"Hector Chavez! What did my dad say to you?" she demanded.

"Calm down, *mamita*. He just wanted to make sure I got more security on you than a three-month-old puppy. And he wanted to share the state of his appeal, which might be looking good for him."

"*What?*" she breathed.

He glanced at her and saw he was right.

She was digging building this slightly-less-fucked-up-but-still-fucked-up new relationship with her father. And it would be easier to do if she didn't have to wait a month between visits.

"He's appealing the sentence, not the verdict, and he might have been handed too strict of one."

"Is that even possible?"

Hector blew out a breath.

Once he'd done that, he shared, "Yeah. It's possible. Judges aren't infallible. In this case, the judge was new. Only appointed six months before Seth's trial. Federal appointment, that's about politics, not ability or experience, or even understanding of the law. Our team was worried we got him, because he seemed like a cowboy jackass who was aiming to make a name for himself, and that could swing both ways. Seth wasn't found guilty on all counts, and gotta admit, we were shocked he got hammered with that big of a sentence. The judge pulled some shit with not allowing evidence during the sentencing phase, and I knew our prosecutor wasn't feeling good about it. Now I know why."

"So what does this mean?"

"His sentence can be reduced to five years, which means he's eligible for parole next year."

"Blooming heck," she mumbled. But more clearly, she asked, "Why wouldn't he want me around when he talked about that?"

"Because he didn't know if you'd take it as good news or bad, and he didn't want to be there if you took it as bad."

"Oh," she whispered, the sadness not lost on him, even with that single syllable.

He held out his hand to her, demanding, "Hand."

She put hers in his.

He curled his fingers around and rested both on his thigh.

"Write to him," he encouraged. "Let him know you're feelin' good about this possible change."

"Okay."

He brought her fingers to his lips and brushed them there.

"Do you still hate him?" she asked quietly.

"I won't, if he gets out and considers his term in prison as indication he should retire. And then he retires. I will, if he causes you any worry, upset, or puts you in danger."

"It'll be interesting to see how that goes," she murmured.

Maybe interesting to her.

Hector was dreading it.

He knew she'd pick him and her new life over her father if it came down to it. Regrettably for Seth, he might have spent years smothering her with his brand of protection to keep her safer than he did her mother, but he hadn't spent those years being a good dad.

But even if she'd been dead for years, for Sadie, she'd essentially just lost her mother.

He didn't want her to lose the last blood family she had left.

Nope.

That wasn't right.

He never wanted her to lose anything she didn't want lost ever again.

In other words, whatever happened, he'd suck it up.

For Sadie.

He came in the back door with Eddie. Jet was there, and Sadie was cooking dinner for all of them.

Eddie barely cleared the door after Hector when they heard shouted, "*Are you high, Claree?*"

Hector stopped and looked to Eddie.

Eddie grinned at Hector.

A five-month-old German shepherd crashed into his shins.

He bent down to give his girl a head rub, agreeing with Sadie.

He missed her floppy ears.

But she was still their gorgeous girl.

"Hola, *mi perrita tan hermosa*," he murmured.

Gretl licked his wrist.

"Ralphie, calm down," they heard Sadie demand.

"Midnight blue and *ice*?" Ralphie asked. "*Ice* isn't even a color."

"Yes, it is!" Tod declared irately. "Look, right there." They heard some pounding, likely on the dining room table. "I only have *seventeen swatches of it.*"

"*Hermano*," Eddie said low, still grinning. "I told you, put her in a plane, marry her in Vegas, and skip the wedding planning."

Sadie had her ring.

Sadie also had her last induction ceremony into the Rock Chicks.

Tod started a wedding planner book for her approximately a nanosecond after they announced they were engaged. And he could do this because he'd already bought a blank one for them. Not only that, but Sadie told him Tod had already added some "preliminary concepts" in it.

Apparently, he and Eddie had walked in while they were engaged in a Rock Chick Gathering, nailing down those concepts.

Hector and Eddie, with Gretl circling around Hector's legs, walked into the kitchen, and Hector saw through the doorway that led to the front of the house that the gang was all there, crowded around the dining room table. So many of them, they'd had to take the stools from the kitchen and still, some asses were sharing seats.

But only Ralphie and Tod were facing off.

"Sadie veritably *screams* pink," Ralphie proclaimed as Hector and his brother made the room and took the only positions they could since the room was so crowded.

They leaned against a wall.

"We already did pink for Indy," Tod sniffed.

"Indy doesn't *own* the color pink," Ralphie returned. "There's ballet pink. And bubblegum pink. And watermelon. And blush. Rose. Mulberry. Carnation. Powder puff. Seashell. Flamingo. Fuchsia. *Oh my God!*" Ralphie shouted, turning to Sadie. "Fuchsia and cobalt blue!"

"Jumpin' Jehoshsphats, *hot pink* would be just plain *hawt*," Annette put in.

"There's also Barbie pink," Roxie said, and Hector hoped like fuck she was joking.

"Wait, isn't Barbie and hot pink the same?" Stella asked.

"Nuances, girl," Indy answered.

"Strawberry!" Daisy shouted out like it was a game to name all the shades of pink. "You could do one of those chocolate fountains, sugar, and have lots and lots of strawberries."

"Whatever it is, it's gotta go with my 'fro," Shirleen decreed. "By that I mean, have a glitter spray that complements it. Though fortunately, with my skin, all shades of pink deliver."

"Hot pink and Prince purple rain. Done. And sofa-king *phat!*" Annette threw up the devil's horns. "Totally rock 'n' roll!"

"Kill me, love of my life," Tod begged Stevie. "Plunge a knife in my heart and end my misery."

"Oh please. Can anyone say *drama*?" Ralphie asked.

"Cobalt blue and *fuchsia*?" Tod shot back.

"I think it's probably best not to remind Tod at this point he suggested chocolate and mustard for Indy," Ally stage-whispered, and Tod's head snapped around.

"It wasn't chocolate and mustard. It was *tangerine* and chocolate."

"Orange and poo, same thing," Ally, ever the shit-stirrer, stirred.

Tod's face got red.

"Hi, babe," Sadie called his way, and the minute she did, Gretl left her place sitting on his feet, panting to go to her mama.

He lifted his chin to her.

Her ice-blue eyes sparkled.

He felt that flare in his gut, spreading warmth.

She was happy. In her element. Surrounded by friends.

Thank fuck he didn't take her to Vegas to get hitched, she would have missed this.

She then turned to Tod. "I like the idea of seashell, Tod. It's opalescent. You can work with that, you know, instead of ice? Right?"

Tod considered it a second, then he chanted, "I'm seeing it, I'm seeing it." He lifted his hands and spread them out like he was envisioning a marquee. "The most delicate iridescent seashell and the fire of...wait for it...*opal!*"

"Oh...my...*gawd!*" Ralphie exclaimed. "It's perfect!"

"Isn't it?" Tod asked.

Ralphie threw his chair back. "Is the fabric store still open?"

"They know me. Even if they're closing, they'll let us nip some swatches while they sweep the floors."

Tod snatched up the planner lying spread out on the table, and he and Ralphie bumped into each other on the way to the front door, but even so, they didn't miss a step.

"Guess I'm going. Love you, girlies," Stevie said, getting up and blowing kisses without using his hand.

"Me too," Buddy put in. He gave Hector a chin lift, one to Eddie, a smile around the table, then as he walked with Stevie to the door, he suggested, "We drop them, make sure they can get in. Then we'll take my truck, go get a beer, and they can meet us for dinner?"

"Works for me," Stevie replied.

Clearly, Tod and Ralphie exiting the room and taking the wedding binder with them meant the Gathering was over.

He knew this when Sadie came to Hector and rested her weight into him where he stood leaning against the wall, arms crossed on his chest.

Gretl, as ever at her mama's side, came with.

"I'm making tacos. Jet says it's easy. Just brown ground beef, throw some water and seasoning in, and *voilà*."

"The food of my people," he teased.

She giggled.

When she was done doing that, she shared, "Ava and Stella already popped out to get more beef and cheese and tortillas. And, um...sour cream and jalapeños and lettuce and other stuff."

His eyes swept the table. "Good call."

Her voice dipped when she asked, "You're not mad it's not just you and your brother, Jet and me?"

"You happy to cook for thirteen people?

"Lee, Hank, Vance, with Max, Mace, Luke, Marcus and Jason are all on their way over."

He started laughing.

She smiled at him while he did.

He circled her with his arms. "What? Not Tex?"

"He said he's setting fire to any wedding planner in his sight from now until Ally gets hitched. So when Jet asked him to pop over tonight, he said he's not coming within five miles of our house if the wedding planner is in it."

"Is Ally getting hitched?" he asked curiously, considering her situation with Ren Zano hadn't yet been outed, at least, not that he knew.

"I don't know, is she?" Sadie asked back, watching him closely.

He shrugged a single shoulder.

She stuck her tongue out at him.

It was an offer he couldn't refuse.

So he kissed her.

Hector stood back.

Sadie moved forward.

And at the base of the pink marble tomb, she rested a spray of gardenias.

She then sat on the step and said, "It's official, mama. Our wedding colors are seashell and opal."

Hector leaned against a tree.

Gretl found her spot and urinated next to a tombstone.

When she was done, she loped to Hector, and they waited as Sadie visited with her mother.

"C'mere," Hector muttered.

Sadie fought the bubbles and drifted across the hot tub toward him.

Even though she'd seen them in it dozens of times, Gretl prowled the deck like she feared them drowning and sporadically barked at the foaming water.

Sadie straddled Hector and wrapped her arms around his neck.

Under the water, he did the same around her back.

"You good?" he asked.

She nodded, trying not to let it show. How happy she was. But it burst from her like a beacon.

"We can wait," he offered.

"What?"

"We can wait," he repeated. "To get married. So your dad can give you away."

Her eyes gleamed, but she bit her lip.

She let it go to ask, "Do you want to wait?"

"I want you to have what you want."

"It's your wedding too."

"Both Malcolm and Tom will come to blows to walk you down the aisle, so to avoid that, Seth filling that spot because it's his wouldn't suck."

It was official.

The appeal had been upheld.

The sentence reduced.

In less than a year, her father would more than likely get parole. He was a model prisoner, and when he wanted to, he could charm a snake. A parole board would be eating out of his hands.

"It's not set in stone he'll get early release. We could be waiting years," Sadie noted.

"You're in my bed, *mi cielo*, your clothes in my closet. Not mine. Ours. This house has been ours since the first time you walked in the door. Fuck knows it is now, since you talked me into yellow cabinets in the kitchen."

"They're butter," she mumbled irritably, the irritation probably coming from remembering the throwdown they'd had about it.

"Whatever," he said on a grin.

"It's clean and sunny and cheerful, and fits the age of the house."

"Right," he muttered.

"Ugh," she grumbled.

He gave her a squeeze. "What I'm saying is, you got my ring on your finger. You got my ink in your skin. You got my commitment. I've got yours. Who cares when we get married? If it's next year or three years from now, you're mine, I'm yours, that's it. A wedding just makes it official."

"I'm not sure I can keep Ralphie and Tod getting along for that length of time. There was a heated discussion about champagne fountains in Art yesterday that nearly caught the place on fire... *again*."

Hector smiled at her.

But...fuck.

He had to do it.

Since it was for her (mostly), he did it.

"It would kill him to miss your wedding."

She pressed her lips together.

Then she ducked her head and moved in, putting them to his ear.

"I love you loads and loads, Hector Chavez."

Yeah.

She knew he did it for her.

Worth it.

He gave her a squeeze, "Love you too, *mi corazón*." He turned his head and returned her gesture, putting his lips to her ear. "Now, lose the bottoms."

Her head went back, and he liked that glitter in the ice of her eyes most of all.

She shifted away just enough to shimmy out of her bottoms.

And then she came right back.

He wanted to leave that room like he wanted someone to drill holes in his head.

But he had to.

He kissed the tops of two heads before he went, heading to the waiting room.

He walked in and all eyes came to him.

"It's a girl. All systems go. Sadie is a fucking warrior," he announced.

Cheers rang up.

Tex boomed, "Fuckin' A, bubba!"

Buddy cracked open a box of cigars.

Ralphie and Tod hugged.

Eddie clapped him on the back then came in for a hug.

He got the same from several dozen more people before he found two sets of eyes.

Those two followed him back to Sadie's room.

The instant she saw them, his mother babbled in Spanish until the tears overtook her, and Hector had to pull her in his arms.

Once *su madre* got her shit together, she got her first.

It was hard to get her away from her grandmother, but he did, then he took her to her grandfather.

Carefully, Hector eased his daughter into Seth's arms.

The man stared down at her like he'd never seen anything so beautiful.

Obviously, he was right.

Nothing in history was as beautiful as the baby Hector and Sadie made.

Seth moved that look to his daughter.

"Lola?" he asked to confirm the name Hector already told them.

"Lola Elizabeth," Sadie whispered the whole thing for the first time.

Hector heard his mother's soft sob.

But he watched the tear slide out of Seth's eye.

"She's perfect," he said gruffly, not taking his gaze from his own girl, and Hector suspected he wasn't the only one in the room who wasn't sure which "she" Seth was referring to.

Hector walked out, eyes to white sand that melted into sparkling turquoise, then azure, then Mediterranean blue.

But mostly they were on the three females playing on the beach.

One, a little black-haired toddler wearing a red and pink polka dot one-piece. One, a curvy strawberry-blonde fairy princess beauty. And the last, his mother.

He handed a bottle of Mythos to the man rocking in the rocker on the porch.

Seth took it and Hector folded into the other rocking chair next to him.

"He good?" Hector asked.

Seth gently patted the diapered bottom of Gus where he lay, on his belly on his granddad's chest, head turned Hector's way, his little pink lips pursed, eyes closed, the wispy black hairs on his head swaying in the breeze.

"He'd sleep through a hurricane," Seth replied.

"Thank fuck," Hector muttered.

Seth chuckled.

They sat in the shade sipping beer in comfortable silence, while the women messed around under a Cretan sun.

Seth broke it.

"I never thanked you. High time I did."

"For what?"

"You know what."

He did.

"I loved her," Hector explained simply.

"Even then?"

Hector took a sip.

When he was done, he replied, "From the minute I laid eyes on her."

"I know that feeling."

Finally, Hector looked to his father-in-law. "I know you do." He gave it a beat, taking in the man beside him, who was no less fit and vital than he'd been the first time Hector met him, and he advised, "You should find someone, man."

Another pat on Gus's diaper and, "I'm an old granddad now."

Not even close.

"You're not even sixty."

Seth's focus sharpened on him. "I think you know, there's only one *one*."

Hector turned to look at Sadie in her ice-blue bikini, swinging

Lola around, both of their laughter mingling and drifting up to the villa.

"Yeah," he agreed. "There's only one *one*."

Hector took another sip of his beer and stretched out his legs.

Seth kept rocking so Gus would keep sleeping.

And the Cretan sun gleamed off the sea.

TRACK 8
ROCK CHICK REVOLUTION

Never in Any Doubt

Ren

Ren opened his eyes to a dark room.

Then he tossed the covers off, angled out of bed and headed downstairs.

He had the kitchen light on and the fridge open by the time she came in the back.

He turned his head to her, doing a quick scan, top to toe.

Seeing no blood, bruising or torn clothing, he relaxed. Not that he'd ever seen any of that, but with her job, the scan had become automatic.

Once he accomplished it, he greeted, "Hey, baby."

"Hey," Ally replied, coming to him.

They touched lips, she reached beyond him, grabbed a Fat Tire and wandered to the drawer where they kept their bottle opener.

She snapped the cap then hefted herself up on her usual place on the counter.

"Baked ziti?" he asked.

"You have a great ass and great eyes and know how to use your dick, but I'd be with you just for your cooking," she said by way of reply, then took a drag off her beer, but he didn't miss her eyes twinkling.

Ren smirked and decided to take that as a yes on the ziti.

He cracked the lid and threw the Tupperware in the microwave.

When it was nuking, he leaned a hip on the counter.

"Tonight go okay?" he asked.

"My brother is a badass."

She was ride-along with Lee that night.

"Know that. Did you learn anything?"

"I learned my brother is more badass than I already knew, and I thought he was a pretty kickass badass already."

Ren crossed his arms on his chest and smiled at her.

She wound her head around to get tension out of her neck, and he didn't like it.

"What?" he pushed quietly.

"It's like, he's forgotten more than I'll ever learn," she told him.

"He's been doing this for years. You've been officially doing it for a couple of months."

"Yeah. I told myself that. Newsflash, it didn't make me feel any better."

Ren felt a heat start burning in his chest. "Lee make you feel like this isn't what you should be doing?"

He asked because he wasn't convinced Lee was fully onboard, even if he said he was. Since he said it, he'd put training and ride-alongs behind that assertion.

Still.

Your little sister enters a game that can be dangerous, even if you say you've got her back, you might still do shit to put her off, even unconsciously.

She shook her head. "No. He was cool. He's patient. It wasn't like I fucked up. It's just...he's such a natural at this shit. He thinks five moves ahead. He's so intuitive, it's like he knows what someone is going to do before they know they're going to do it."

"Again, he's been doing this longer than you. You'll get to that place."

"I—"

He cut her off gently. "Don't."

She shut her mouth.

"This is what you want," Ren reminded her. "This is who you are. You're going to have times like these. Times where you question yourself. You gotta shake that off and keep going."

She held his gaze for long beats.

Then she whispered, "My champion."

"Fuck yeah," he whispered back.

She smiled the famous Nightingale smile at him.

The microwave binged.

Ren walked across the hall and entered Ally's offices to see if she wanted to head out and get a quick lunch.

He stopped inside the door when he saw Tex's enormous back, seeing as Tex was standing in front of Daisy's desk, all but obscuring it.

And Daisy didn't have a small desk.

He also looked to Ally's office, which had a wall of windows.

She wasn't there.

"It's not like she's gotta pay my insurance," Tex boomed, bringing Ren's attention back to them. "Indy's got that covered. She's just gotta throw me some action once in a while. In case you haven't noticed, woman, shit around here has gotten boring."

"I hear you, sugar," Daisy replied. "But it isn't like her cases all have high-speed chases and shootouts."

Thank fuck, Ren thought.

"A lot of times it's staking someone out and waiting for your shot to close in and take pictures of someone doin' the nasty," Daisy went on.

"Want no part in that," Tex mumbled (but somehow, it was still a boom).

Daisy's tinkling laughter sounded. "I hear that too. I see the pictures. Me and my Marcus went to this place that had a lot of mirrors once, and I was sure to get prepared. Good hair. Full face of makeup. Glitter dust on my skin. The nasty is just *nasty* if you don't go in prepared."

Tex's hand shot up. "Too much information," he growled.

Ren agreed.

He also walked forward.

Tex swung around and Daisy smiled at Ren. She did it the way only Daisy can do it...huge. "Hey there, honey bunches of oats."

"Hey, Daisy," he replied, and looked to the big man. "Tex."

"Zano."

"I take it Ally isn't here?" he asked Daisy.

"Due back soon. Want me to send her over?"

"Would you? If she has time, wanna take my woman to lunch."

"Love to, darlin'."

He nodded to her, lifted his chin to Tex, then he headed back to his office.

When he got there, their new receptionist, Sarah, who was quiet, pretty, in her mid-forties, and very good at her job, immediately said, "I'm sorry, Mr. Zano. I tried to stop him."

Shit.

"But your uncle is here. He's in your office," she finished.

Fantastic.

"I really did try to stop him," she went on.

"It's okay, Sarah," he assured. "He's unstoppable if he wants to be."

She appeared relieved he understood.

Ren headed to his office.

Vito didn't get up when he hit it, just turned in his chair and watched as Ren walked to his desk.

He sat behind it and didn't get a word in before Vito spoke.

"Father Paolo says Ally's takin' Catholic classes."

Ren nodded. "She is."

"Good," he grunted.

Vito said no more.

Neither did Ren.

They hadn't spoken since the big blowup. Even though Vito was sitting right there, Ren knew it was going to have to be him who officially extended the olive branch. Vito was too damned stubborn to do it. It just pissed him off it had to be him.

But family was family.

Vito taught him that.

He opened his mouth.

Vito beat him to it again.

"You know," Vito began, "before we got married, Angela and me named all our kids."

Ren felt something tighten in his chest since he knew with this opener it was story time from Vito, he just wasn't going to like this story. He also knew, when Vito was in the mood to tell a story, he had no choice but to sit back and listen.

So he did that.

"We picked eight names. The middle name and everything," Vito shared. "Not that we wanted eight kids. We wanted four. But, you know, you never know what a kid's gonna come out like. We figured we'd have to have alternates just in case an Antonio turned out to be a Massimo."

"Right," Ren said quietly.

"We gave it time in the beginning. I just wanted Angela. She just wanted me. But we knew when we were gonna add on. We had it all planned. We had years, we thought, to make our family."

Vito and Angela were childless.

Yeah, he knew he wasn't going to like this story.

"Vito," Ren whispered.

It was like he didn't speak.

Vito continued.

"When the time came, months went by. Years. Nothin'. Took her to doctors, every one we could find in Denver. One in LA. One in San Francisco. Two in New York. One in DC."

Christ.

"It was just not gonna happen," he carried on. "They all said the same things. Even when science advanced, it wouldn't have happened. My Angela just didn't have something down there that worked right."

Ren said nothing.

"She tried to leave me."

Ren said something to that.

"Jesus."

Vito was a family man. He was also Italian. He was powerful, and he was wealthy.

But Ren had never even seen him look at another woman other than his wife.

He and Vito had a father-son relationship, and Vito didn't share about that kind of thing. But Ren would be shocked stupid if Vito had ever stepped out on Angela.

He loved her. Doted on her.

Dom could be an ass, but Vito hadn't given up on him, until Dom started cheating on Sissy. That was something he couldn't abide, a character flaw that Vito found indefensible. Ren agreed.

It also gave further evidence to the thought that Vito would never do that to his own wife, and not because God said you shouldn't cheat.

Because he respected her too much.

He loved her too much.

And just that she was the only woman he wanted.

"She knew I wanted kids as bad as she did," Vito kept going. "The problem wasn't with me. It was with her. She thought if I was free to find another woman, I'd have what I needed most in this world. It was the hardest blow I've ever sustained."

Ren again said nothing, but this time, he didn't because of the look that came into his uncle's eyes.

"I fell down on the job, son. That my Angela would ever...*ever* think I needed anything else in this world. I died a little death when she said that to me. I still haven't recovered, and she said that shit to me thirty years ago. Hear me, Lorenzo, make certain your woman knows, without ever questioning, that there is not one thing on this earth you need more than her at your side."

"Think you already taught me that, Uncle Vito," Ren murmured.

Again, it was like Ren didn't speak.

"You're my boy," Vito said softly. "You all grown up, not wantin' to do what I did, makin' it plain you didn't wanna be grown up and be like me. That was the second hardest blow I ever took."

Goddamn fuck.

"Vito—"

His uncle raised his hand. "I get it. Talked with Angela about it. She told me what a stubborn ass I am and that I did what I did for the reasons I did it. But I'm not you. Any good father lets their son choose his own path. It isn't an indictment if they don't choose yours. It's a gift you got to give. And I fell down again because I didn't give it."

"I should have been more sensitive to you bein' in that place," Ren replied.

Vito shook his head. "It's on me to show you the way. You and Ally, you're gonna have kids. You gotta know the way. That's the only path it's on me to show you. You're young. Got your life ahead of you. It's not on you to make shit easy on me. It's on me to show you the way."

"You showed me the way, Uncle Vito," he said low.

This time, Vito nodded his head. "Proud of you, son. Proud of your cousin for gettin' his head out of his ass and turnin' his attention to his wife, where it should be. Wasn't sure he had that in him. He's a lucky guy, she gave him a second chance. But you, Lorenzo. I've always been proud of you."

Fuck it.

Ren stood and walked around the desk.

Vito stood and turned to Ren.

When Ren got close, Vito's hand shot out, curved around the back of Ren's neck, and he yanked him into his body, wrapping his other arm around. Ren took the same hold, neck and back, and as men do, they both pounded the love into each other's shoulder blades.

The door opened.

They broke and looked that way.

Ally was backing out. "I'll just come back."

Vito clapped his hands. "Nope! I'm gone. Said what had to be said." He clamped his hand on the side of Ren's neck and squeezed while looking into his eyes.

Ren smirked.

"Love you too, Uncle Vito," he said.

Vito nodded once, let Ren go, walked to the door, stopped so Ally could kiss his cheek, then he was gone.

Ally didn't move into the room after the door closed behind him when she asked, "You okay?"

"He was hurt I didn't want to follow in his footsteps."

Understanding lit on her face. "Ah."

"He's over it now."

"Good."

Ren tipped his head to the side. "Is there some reason you're standing all the way over there?"

"Yes. Because I feel the need to comfort you, which will lead to us fucking on your desk again, and I'm hungry. A miracle has happened. I'm so hungry, I want to eat instead of fuck. Or, at least, before we fuck. Does this mean we're turning into an old, staid, boring couple?"

He moved her way, grinning and saying, "No. It just means you're hungry." He put his hands to her hips when he arrived at her. "And just sayin', stomach rumbles are a turn off, baby."

She smiled at him.

He took her in.

He'd had dreams too.

Dreams, actually, of finding a woman like Angela.

A woman like Sissy.

Quiet and supportive, happy to keep house and plan parties and build her life around her man.

His first indication that wasn't what was truly in his heart was when he became attracted to Ava.

The definite proof was when Ally walked out on him because he struggled with holding on to a dream that wasn't ever his. It was Vito's.

His dream was standing right in front of him, sass and fire and strength, and so much love, her every move was guided by it.

"Why are you staring at me like that?" she asked.

"Because Vito and I talked about something else. Now I realize how much I fucked up when I fell down on the job."

"Fell down on what job?"

"The job of making sure you know, and you're never in any doubt, that there is not one thing I need on this earth more than having you at my side."

She leaned into him and whispered, "Ren."

Christ, he loved it when she said his name like that.

Especially when it came with her beautiful face getting soft like that.

Just for him.

She had a lot of love to give.

But that was all his.

"So, I'm going to say it now and do my damnedest to show it from now on. But that's where I'm at."

"We had a hiccup, it's over," she asserted.

"I nearly lost you, and we're not getting lunch until you know I'm not gonna fuck up like that again."

"It isn't about the fact I'm seriously hungry that I share, I already know that, Ren Zano, and I'm not in any doubt."

"Good," he grunted.

"Though, you're gonna have to get over the stomach rumbles."

"Why?"

She started pushing him backward. "Because you're being so sweet, I need to blow you."

He smiled down at her, not about to argue.

So he didn't.

Rock Chick Rewind – Hit Play

Darius

Some time ago...

Ally collapsed on the couch at his side.

"Ugh," she groaned.

Darius turned his head and grinned at her. "What?"

"Look at them," she said, throwing out her hand. "I wish they would just get together already."

Darius looked, but he knew what she was talking about. He'd been watching this shit play out for a long time.

Indy was flirting with Brian Archer, doing this to rile Lee. Although she was too into doing it that she didn't notice she was achieving her goal: Lee was staring at Archer like he wanted to rip his head off.

Indy had the patience of a gnat. If she'd stop trying so hard to get

Lee to notice her, she'd notice he was all about her, and she just had to wait for him to make his move.

Good or bad, guys needed it like that.

At least, guys like Lee.

"She's fourteen," Darius pointed out.

"So?" Ally, also fourteen, asked.

"He's gotta wait at least until she's eighteen."

"Why?"

Darius fake leered at her.

"Gross!" she shouted.

Darius started laughing.

She put her hands to her ears. "La, la, la, not thinking about that."

"You're the one who came over here, complainin' about them getting together."

"Yeah, *Darius*," she said his name like "duh," and he fought busting a gut laughing.

Shit, Ally Nightingale was funny.

He loved her. It was a brother-sister type of love, but even if he was seventeen and she was fourteen, he felt it in a way he knew it'd never die.

"But that's about me," she concluded.

Now he was confused. "What?"

"They get together, stay together and get married, she's my real sister, and, like, we'll spend Christmases and vacations together."

"You already do that."

"Well, some other guy takes her and whisks her off to some boondocks, I won't get to do that anymore, will I?" she returned.

"India Savage is never gonna live in the boondocks," he replied. "And she's never gonna leave you."

Or Lee, he didn't add, but if anyone knew that, Ally did.

"Whatever," she muttered. "We need someone to go out and score some beer."

"We're in your mom and dad's basement."

"And?"

"And your dad is a cop and he's sitting upstairs, watching TV."

She rolled her eyes.

Rarely did Ally let that get in her way, except when she was under her father's roof.

He had this thought as he noticed movement across the room.

He shifted his attention there and watched Hank, down from school in Boulder for the weekend, stick his head in the door. He whistled then gestured to Lee. Lee stopped staring murder at Archer and went to the door. Hank repeated this with Eddie. Eddie quit jacking around pretending not to flirt with Jaclyn Johnson while still flirting so good, he was going to get in her pants soon, and he followed Lee.

Darius waited for his summons. Hank's face had been weird.

What was weirder was the summons didn't come.

The door closed behind Eddie and that was it.

"Sooooooo," Ally drew that out, also drawing Darius's attention. "Malia Clark. You two are hot and heavy, hunh?"

"Gonna marry her," Darius said without hesitation, and he shook off the weird feeling he got from the look he saw on Hank's face, the fact Lee and Eddie got the call, but he didn't, and he was never left out, and he grinned big at Ally's huge eyes.

Mostly, he grinned big thinking about Malia.

"She's smart. She's classy. She's beautiful," he explained.

"Check. Check. And check. But, dude...*married?*"

"Not like...*now*. After I get back from Yale and she finishes getting her law degree. Okay, maybe before she finishes that. We can get married when she's in law school."

Ally stretched out her lips. "Yikes. You have it all planned out."

He did.

His dad told him he knew, the minute he met Darius's mom. He knew that was the only woman for him.

Darius didn't get it when his dad said it.

Until he met Malia.

One thing he did get, and always got, was that he was totally like his dad.

"I like you two together," Ally said quietly. "You're sweet. She's sweet. You're good-looking, or as good-looking as my brother from another mother can be."

He shot her another grin.

"She's gorgeous. Perfect match," she finished.

"Yeah," he agreed, distracted because the door opened again, and Eddie came through.

But he didn't fully come in.

He stepped to the side and Lee filled the doorway.

They both had eyes to him, and he liked the looks on their faces a whole lot less than the one that was on Hank's.

"Hey, bro, can you come upstairs a second?" Lee called.

"What's going on?" Ally asked.

"Don't know," Darius said, pushing out of the couch.

Ally came up with him.

"Just Darius, yeah, *cariño*?" Eddie said to Ally, all gentle like.

And...*damn*.

Eddie didn't pull out the *cariño* for anybody.

Ally must have felt that too, because for once, Ally did what someone asked rather than doing whatever the hell she wanted.

Lee walked partly up the steps to get out of his way before Darius stopped in the small landing at the foot of the stairs at the door to the rec room. Eddie came into the space, crowding him and closing the door behind him.

"What's up?" he asked.

"Just..." Lee's voice sounded choked. "Come upstairs," he finished, like he was forcing out the words.

Nope.

Darius didn't like this shit at all.

They got up the stairs and into the kitchen, and he liked this less.

He noticed it all, all at once.

He did this knowing, even if he lived to be a hundred, he'd never forget it.

Not any of it.

Hank was shoulders against the back wall, arms crossed on his chest, ankles crossed, head bent so deep, Darius couldn't see his face.

Tom was sitting at the table.

His eyes came right to Darius.

His face was ravaged.

Malcolm was standing, holding Kitty Sue.

Kitty Sue was silently crying.

Malcolm looked wrecked.

Darius's insides seized.

"What's up?" he repeated, but this time his voice was small.

Because he knew.

His mom.

One of his sisters.

Maybe an accident.

It was something like that.

Something bad.

Kitty Sue stepped out of Malcolm's hold and called, "Honey, come here."

He didn't go there.

He backed up and ran into a wall that was made of Lee and Eddie.

One of them grabbed a fistful of his T-shirt.

The other wrapped his hand around the back of Darius's neck.

Fuck, he knew.

This was *bad*.

The adults, they didn't know. They didn't know how to deal.

And two of them were fucking cops.

It was Hank.

It was Hank who lifted his head, looked Darius in his eyes, and the infinite sorrow and pain and love in his made Darius's knees weak.

And then Hank opened his mouth and said words that changed Darius forever.

Fast Forward – Hit Play

His boy approached, wearing cap and gown.

He went to his momma first.

She hugged him and the tears fell silently from her eyes.

They held on a good while before Liam touched his forehead to hers, smiled at her, let her go and then bent to pick up his baby sister.

"Congradlations, LeeLee!" she shouted.

Liam grinned at her, let her hug him and give him a wet kiss on his cheek.

Then he put her down and turned to his father.

Darius waited for him to make the move.

He did.

Liam wrapped his arms around his dad and pounded him on the back.

Darius returned the gesture.

"Proud of you," Darius muttered.

"Yeah. Proud of you too."

Darius swallowed.

Liam held on.

"Oh my God, stop hugging. If you don't, I won't stop crying, and I'm hungry. I need to eat," Malia demanded.

Darius and Liam both leaned back, but they didn't let go.

They just smiled at each other.

Only then did they let go.

Liam claimed his baby sister again, planting her on his hip.

Darius claimed his wife.

They followed their kids to the car.

And then Darius Tucker took his family to dinner.

Fast Forward – *Way* Forward – Hit Play

Jimmy Marker

Jimmy'd had the bottle a long time.

A long...*fucking*...time.

He took it from the place it had inhabited for years at the back of the fridge, got the glasses and walked out on the deck where his wife was sitting.

She looked to the bottle, the glasses, then to her husband.

"No," she said, not believing it.

It had been years.

But now...it was official.

He sat, put the glasses down on their patio table, and started to take the foil off the two-hundred-and-fifty-dollar bottle of champagne.

"Jorge called," he said.

"From Phoenix?" she asked.

"Yup."

Jimmy's friend, and ex-colleague, Jorge Alvarez, was now in Phoenix.

In fact, Jorge moved down there fifteen years ago, and now he was Chief of Police in Phoenix.

Jimmy threw the foil on the table and went after untwisting the wire.

"Cap Jackson moved down there. He's gonna be part of the new NI setup. Their new branch."

His wife appeared confused. "Cap Jackson? Is he any relation to Roam and Sniff?"

"Yup." Jimmy popped the cork and started pouring while explaining, "Seeing as he *is* Sniff. Kid got back from the Army and he's no kid anymore. You might try to call him Sniff if you wanted your face rearranged. They called him Cap in the military, not because of his rank. Short for Captain America. And not just because he's strong, loyal and fearless. But because he looks like Chris Evans, and word got 'round about the scrawny bugger he used to be. The name stuck when he got back."

His wife fought a smile as she said, "Oh boy."

"Oh boy is right," Jimmy agreed. "And Jorge tells me some vigilante, calling themselves the 'Avenging Angel,' is doin' stupid shit in Phoenix."

"Oh boy," his wife repeated, her eyes lighting.

"Yup," Jimmy said yet again, putting the bottle down, picking up both the glasses and handing one to his wife. "Jorge suspects this Avenging Angel is female."

She was losing the fight with her smile.

Jimmy kept talking.

"And as we both know, Phoenix isn't even in the same fucking state as Denver. So way, *way* out of my jurisdiction."

His woman lost it and started laughing.

Jimmy offered his glass for a clink. His wife reached out and clinked.

"Here's to Jorge having a shit ton of patience. Here's to that shit happening down there and not up here. And here's to it finally being over."

"And here's to new adventures in true love," she returned.

"Whatever," he muttered.

She kept laughing even as she drank, which meant she started choking.

Christ, his wife was a goof.

But fuck, he loved her.

TRACK 9
ROCK CHICK REAWAKENING

Batman

Marcus

"Where's my wife?" he asked Conchita, their housekeeper, when she poked her head out of one of the rooms as he walked down the hall of his home.

"Upstairs, Mr. Sloan. Your bedroom."

He nodded and headed that way.

He heard the voices before he got there because the door was open.

But he knew they were there because of the car that was outside.

So he stopped in the door, rested his shoulder on the jamb and just stood there, watching.

His wife was on the bed. She had one of her marabou trim robes on, the blue one. She also had her hair held back in a wide, white band and her face covered in something purple.

Roxie was also there. She too was wearing one of Daisy's robes, without marabou, and her face was covered in something white.

Last, Annette was there. It was no surprise she picked a marabou robe, and she had on a pair of Daisy's high-heeled, feathered slippers, even though they didn't fit her feet, so her heel was hanging over an inch. Her face was covered in something green.

All three were in a line on their backs, their legs straight and up, heels resting on the headboard.

Daisy was speaking. "It drains the nodes."

"What nodes?" Annette asked.

"I don't know what nodes, sugar, I'm no doctor. I just know, you sit like this for a good ten, twenty minutes, the swelling in your feet goes down," Daisy shared. "And it also feels good. Energizing-like. But in a relaxing way."

"Though, the swelling's not gonna go down so much your size eights change into Daisy's size sixes," Roxie warned, clearly referring to Annette's feet in the slippers.

"I know I should care that probably some birds lost their lives for these feathers, but I feel like such a *girl* in them," Annette declared. "It's *phat*."

"I hear that, sister," Daisy said. "I got a strict rule. Feathers, but no fur. I know birds got rights too, but a girl's gotta draw the line somewhere and still get her pretty things."

A rule, one of many, Daisy lived by.

"Don't tell Jason I wore this robe," Annette ordered.

Annette's partner was a vegetarian.

Marcus heard his wife's extraordinary laugh. He also, like always, felt it in the left side of his chest.

"Your secret's safe with us," she assured.

"I can feel my face morphing," Annette announced. "It's like I'm ten years younger already."

"That's the point, darlin'," Daisy told her. "Though, it ain't *the truth*, it's the point. Doin' nice things for yourself makes you feel like a million bucks."

"Amma used to be my guru, you're my guru now," Annette declared.

"Let Amma keep your spirit, sugar," Daisy advised. "I'll take care of your skin."

"Deal!" Annette exclaimed, punching the air as her exclamation point.

Again, he heard his wife's laughter.

Silently, Marcus moved out of the doorway.

It was girl time for Daisy.

All her life, she'd wanted girls to share facials and feet-swelling remedies with.

Now she had them.

It wasn't like he felt he was intruding, and not just because it would upset Daisy greatly if she knew he thought that way.

It was that, a person like Daisy, who had the love Daisy had to give, and who deserved all the love she could get, having that hole in her life all her life...she had some making up to do.

It was fortunate the Rock Chicks gave sisterhood better than any other.

They'd make that up in no time at all.

Indeed, maybe they already had.

He still left them to it.

Because Daisy deserved a lot of love.

And the Rock Chicks did too.

They were at the breakfast table and his wife had just slid his plate in front of him.

He'd kept in shape before her with daily workouts.

When she entered his life, he adjusted his eating schedule where lunches were light, or he just had a protein drink, and he added a half an hour to his workouts. He did this because her Southern breakfasts had also entered his life.

"Thank you, darling," he murmured, picking up his fork when she sat down. After he swallowed his first bite, he asked, "What are your plans for today?"

"Got a scheduled RCG at Fortnum's this mornin'," she answered, scooping up some of her hash brown casserole.

RCG was the acronym for Rock Chick Gathering. These were unofficially official meetings of the Rock Chicks.

However unofficial, attendance was mandatory.

"What's this one about?" Marcus asked, hiding his disappointment, something he'd become adept at doing.

It was Saturday.

He wanted her to have girl time, but since the Rock Chicks came into her life, it sometimes interrupted their couple time.

"We're headin' off Rock-Chick-Eggedon."

He chuckled, even not knowing what this was about.

Sadie and Hector's wedding date was set now that Seth's release date was set.

Ally had Ren's ring on her finger.

No one's apartment had exploded, or business had burned down now for months.

So he figured "Rock-Chick-Eggedon" was not something he truly had to worry about.

Not anymore.

When Daisy explained, she proved him right.

"We got a situation happening between Kitty Sue, Ally and Indy. See, Kitty Sue wants to host Ally's shower. But Ally doesn't want a shower. She says Ren's all set up and he does the cooking and his towels are real nice, so she doesn't need any shower type stuff. She said he even has a champagne bucket, so, you know, that there's proof positive the man is *set*. Ally just wants a bachelorette party. This, I think, is code for her not wantin' her momma to throw a shower for her that requires attendees to bring lingerie. Ally's weird about sex like that."

Marcus ate, listening and smiling.

"Now, at the same time, we got Indy, who is down with letting Kitty Sue have shower duties, but ain't no way she's gonna let Kitty Sue horn in on the bachelorette planning action. So she needs Ally to let her mom throw a shower so she can be clear to throw the bachelorette party. 'Cause Kitty Sue decreed she's throwin' *somethin'* for her girl. She don't care what it is. And she's a momma, so what she says goes."

"What do you think is going to happen?" he asked while she took a sip of coffee.

Daisy put her cup down. "Ally will cave and let her mom throw the shower, mostly 'cause Ren's like you. He's visual as well as tactile in the sex department, so she needs as many sexy nighties and teddies as she can get. That'll free Indy to do her bachelorette mojo. Then all will be well again in the world of the Rock Chicks."

"So really, Ally just needs to stop being stubborn."

"Yeah, so that's probably gonna take us through about three of Tex's lattes, 'cause that girl's got a chokehold on stubborn."

Marcus chuckled and continued to eat.

It took him a while to realize Daisy didn't fill the silence.

He turned his attention from his plate to her.

The instant he did, she asked, "What you doin' today, honey bunches of love?"

He'd wanted to spend it with her. Maybe take her to a movie. Out to lunch. Spend the day in bed like they used to, ordering in food when they needed it, but mostly just feeding off what they already had. Each other.

"I think I'll go to the club. See if I can find a foursome to play with."

Her head tipped to the side and so did her pretty hair.

Her eyes also narrowed.

"You like golf, Marcus?" she asked a good question, since he'd taken it up only recently.

And actually, he detested it.

But he liked being outside. It worked muscles in a way he didn't work them in the gym. It was a personal challenge, attempting to better his game, and Marcus liked challenges. And he didn't mind strolling the eighteen lanes.

"Of course," he semi-lied.

Her eyes stayed narrowed.

"Meet you at the club for a late lunch," he suggested.

"I don't know..." she started slowly. "I might have plans for lunch."

"Then we'll go out somewhere for dinner."

"That sounds good," she said, like her thoughts were far away.

"Eat, baby," he urged. "You don't want to be late for the Gathering."

"Right," she mumbled.

Marcus cleaned his plate. Daisy gave him the warning look she always gave him when he made a move to take it to the sink.

Through his wife, he knew no one cleaned the table of a Southern woman, except that Southern woman.

Even so, he'd never take her for granted.

But as she wished, he left it where it was, kissed her cheek, and also left her finishing her coffee.

He needed to find a golf shirt.

He clocked them first on the ninth hole.

Then again on the tenth, eleventh, twelfth and thirteenth.

It was the fourteenth when club personnel nabbed them.

It was on the fifteenth when a member of staff came and apologized for interrupting his game before asking him if he wouldn't mind accompanying him to the clubhouse.

Marcus left his foursome and accompanied him.

The man led him to the membership office, stopped outside the closed door, smiled and rather nervously said, "This is an unusual situation, Mr. Sloan. Normally, our members know the rules and follow them. In this case, the rule that states you can't be on the course unless you have a tee time. Also, members need to sign in non-members if they're using our facilities. So Mrs. Sloan and her...er... *companions*...erm...*activities* on the course are somewhat frowned upon. We were hoping you might have a word with her."

"I will. Thank you for your discretion."

"Always a pleasure, Mr. Sloan," the man said and scooted away.

Marcus took in a breath before he opened the door.

Shirleen was sitting behind the desk, her feet on top of it, her Louboutin heels on display.

Daisy, Ava and Sadie, the skulking culprits, were sitting in the chairs in front of it, an extra one having been brought in so Sadie could use it.

He could see they'd either divested themselves of their camouflage, or it was confiscated.

"It wasn't me," Shirleen announced. "I was havin' a drink at the bar while they were doin' their silly-ass nonsense."

"Marcus—" Daisy started.

"Ladies," he cut her off, addressing Ava, Sadie and Shirleen. "Do you have rides or do you need me to arrange them for you?"

Shirleen took her feet off the desk. "That means get the fuck out, I got words to say to my wife."

It absolutely did.

Shirleen stood, "I brought 'em all here. I can take them back. I assume you'll take Daisy home?"

"You assume correctly," Marcus confirmed.

Slowly, Ava and Sadie stood, giving Daisy "I'm sorry" expressions as they trooped behind Shirleen out the door.

Sadie still had a leaf stuck in the back of her hair.

He waited until it closed, then he shifted his position to lean against it and face his wife.

"Marcus—" she started again.

"Please begin by explaining why you're spying on me."

"I wasn't spying. You're my husband. You can't spy on your husband," she returned.

"When you're wearing a makeshift camo hat with branches stuck in it and lurking through trees on a golf course, watching me when you think I don't know you're there, that's spying."

She pressed her lips tightly together.

It took effort to keep the bite out of his voice when he demanded. "What is it, Daisy? Do you think I'm cheating on you?"

This was the only thing he could dredge up as explanation for her behavior, considering the foursome he'd joined included two women.

She jumped to her feet and cried, "What? No!"

"Then why on earth would you...and Ava...and Sadie...shove branches in knit caps, don safari shirts and creep through trees watching me?"

She threw her hands out to her sides and snapped, "Because I love you."

"I know you do. You don't have to prove it by keeping an eye on me every moment of my life."

"Take your own advice, darlin'," she shot back.

He stiffened.

"Your life can't be just me," she went on.

Marcus stood stone still and silent.

Daisy didn't.

"In the beginning, I needed it. Lord knew, and definitely you did, that I needed a good man's attention and his love and devotion. You give your heart, Marcus, and *God*, there's so much in there to give. All for me. But I can't hack it. It's not fair."

She walked to him and put both hands on his chest (and he noted she might have been skulking through the rough around six holes of golf, and she might have somehow found a safari outfit to do it in, but she'd also managed to find some camo-covered platform boots to wear with it).

"The time has gone when I need you to give me your everything, Marcus," she concluded.

"I realize you have the Rock Chicks now and—"

"I'm not talking about the Rock Chicks. I'm talking about the rape."

Marcus clamped his mouth shut and gritted his teeth.

She noticed and cupped his jaw in her hand. "Life is life, sugar bunch. You can't shield me from it. You can't cushion every fall I might take. And you can't live your life in the wings like you're Batman waitin' for the Bat Signal to come out so you can be available to swoop to my rescue anytime I might need you. You gotta have your own life. Not one without me, but one that's about you so it can be as full as it should be. And you'd be givin' that to me too. Because I want it for you."

"I have a full life, Daisy."

She dropped her hand and stepped back. "You have no friends."

"I don't need friends."

"Okay, then, I'll remind you, you're not in that business anymore where you gotta always be lookin' over your shoulder and wonderin' if every person you deal with is gonna turn around and fuck you over. I'll also remind you, there are some damn fine men in our midst. They respect you. They like you. Hell, darlin', you could take your pick, and I bet they'd welcome you."

"I'm not a beer and wings and football person."

"Heads up, Marcus. Those boys like their sports, sure, but most of their downtime they spend sittin' at Lincoln's, drinkin' beer and wonderin' where they went wrong, gettin' involved with a crazy group of bitches like us. And I'm sure you might have a few things to say on that matter yourself."

His tone was gentle when he told her the absolute truth. "I never wonder why I'm with you."

"I bet you wondered why I was there when some lunatic chased my friends down in a haunted house."

He had to admit, he definitely wondered that.

"Or nearly rolled onto I-25 when someone was chasin' Ava's Range Rover."

And absolutely that.

"Or when someone had to pull me off Harvey Balducci when I was beatin' his stupid ass in the alley behind a gay bar."

He didn't really have to wonder about that.

"Or when Roxie and I got shot at when that bad man from Chicago's boys were on our ass through the streets of Denver."

He didn't even want to think of that.

"Stop talking," he ordered.

"See?" she said like she'd proven her point. "What do you think the men are doing when an RCG is going on?"

"I don't know. Drinking raw eggs before taking Krav Maga classes?"

Her laugh filled the room, and she shook her head. "No, sugar. They're havin' HBAs."

"What's an HBA?"

"A Hot Bunch Assembly, where they hang at Lincoln's, or one or the other's houses, shooting the shit and makin' bets on stuff that don't matter, and silently hoping that Tex isn't gonna be given a reason to craft another makeshift bomb."

He smiled at her.

She didn't smile back.

"You're a member of the Hot Bunch, honey," she told him in all seriousness. "All you gotta do is join the club officially."

He felt something he didn't understand, because it had been so long since he felt it.

It came to him.

Uncomfortable.

"I've never really been a joiner," he admitted.

She approached again, putting her hands back on his chest and leaning into him.

He loved everything about his wife.

But he wasn't so sure about the look in her eye.

"Don't you worry, honey bunches of love. Leave that part to me."

Right, then...

Fuck.

His intercom in the office buzzed.

He hit it. "Yes, Sarah?"

"Mr. Nightingale is here for his appointment."

"Bring him back."

"Right away, Mr. Sloan."

Marcus wasn't sure what this was about. He and Ren still had NI on retainer for various things, but it wasn't like the relationship Marcus used to have with Lee and his men.

And Lee had made this appointment.

So it was either Daisy meddling after their conversation at the club last weekend.

Or it was Lee coming to tell him that his client list had expanded beyond his current capacity, so he needed to drop a few of his less challenging ones.

He wondered what Ren would think of moving those issues to Ally.

The door opened and Sarah ushered Lee in.

"Coffee? Sparkling water? Regular water?" she offered.

"I'm good," Lee said, moving in to shake Marcus's hand.

Marcus had stood and rounded the desk to do the same.

"We both are, Sarah," he told her, "Thank you."

She nodded and stepped out, closing the door behind her.

He gestured to a chair in front of his desk and said, "Have a seat."

Lee sat.

Marcus returned behind his desk and started it.

"What's up?"

"I need some advice."

That wasn't what he expected.

"What kind of advice?"

"I'm hiring two more men. The demand is too much and coming so often, I worry I'm leaving money on the table, so I'm getting back into security. To see to current client loads, and add that back to our menu of services, I not only need to upgrade current equipment, I need more space."

"All right," Marcus replied when Lee paused.

"So I got three choices at the moment. Find another office. Wait and hope the tenants next to my current one vacate and take over their space, which obviously is not optimal, but it might be doable. Or last, buy the whole building, seeing as the property management team told us that the owners were about to put it on the market, so they were feeling out their tenants to offer the opportunity to buy."

Marcus knew what he'd do. He just didn't know if Lee had the capital to do it, or the credit to leverage it.

Therefore, he asked, "Are you in a position to buy?"

"No. Got a new baby. New house. I got money in the bank, but it'd wipe me out if I bought in cash. And not feeling having that kind of debt on top of adding property management on the list of shit to oversee."

"You get a good property management firm, it shouldn't take much of your time at all."

Lee smiled. "Yeah, I know one of those."

Real estate was the bulk of a variety of interests he and Ren managed.

Marcus smiled back. "We'd be happy to take your building on. It'll be a nice change, me looking out for your interests for a while."

"Thanks, man. But I'm not there yet."

"I don't want to add weight to an already weighty decision, especially with your expanding responsibilities including an expanding family. But it'll be a very good investment."

"I got one more option open to me, it's the one I'm leaning toward taking, but it's the one that concerns me the most."

"And it is?"

"Luke, Vance and Hector all said they'd buy in."

"I see," Marcus murmured.

"Mace is probably gonna be on the road a lot with Stella, and they might be moving to LA. But he wants a buy in too."

"What are we talking?"

"I'll always be controlling at fifty-two percent. They'll take a quarter each of the rest."

"Are you okay with giving up forty-eight percent?"

"It means they're tied to the operation, and since I never want to lose any of them, abso-fucking-lutely."

Marcus smiled.

He then asked, "And are they in position to give you enough to buy the building?"

"Luke and Mace are. Hector and Vance are going to get second mortgages on their houses, though Sadie might circumvent that for Hector. She's got the cash to give him. He's just gotta stop thinking with his dick and let his woman be a part of their financial situation."

"Regardless if Hector figures it out, no way around it, with all of them investing, more weight lands on you," Marcus surmised.

Lee nodded. "I can't fuck this up. They do that, too much is riding on it."

"That isn't your problem."

"It is when it's family."

"Yes, true," Marcus whispered.

"So what would you do?" Lee asked.

Well.

Damn.

This wasn't about Daisy setting this up.

This was about respect. This was about the fact that Lee thought highly of him and honestly wanted his advice.

And Marcus felt something else he hadn't felt in a long time, unless Daisy was making him feel that way.

Good.

"You, nor those men, are stupid, Lee. I believe there's a part of them that's investing in you because they believe in you, and they know you're solid. But they also have women and families, or they will, so they're not going to do something to put those important parts of their lives in jeopardy. To end, they believe in this as an investment. They believe it will have fruitful returns. And I believe they're right. Take on these partners. And buy that building."

Characteristically, Lee thought on this for only half a second.

And then he said, "That's what I'll do. Thanks, man."

"My pleasure."

Lee looked over his shoulder at the door, then to his watch, then to Marcus. "Close to quitting time," he noted.

"You're my last appointment."

Lee grinned. "Wanna go out and get a drink?"

For a second, Marcus didn't move.

Then he started laughing.

"Daisy?" he asked.

Lee started laughing too. "Gotta say, Marcus, when she marched her stonewash-denim-clad ass in my office and told me to be friends with you, I was half scared of her, half wondering if someone time warped me back to middle school to Mrs. Zhang's class, a real ball-buster, when she made me be friends with all the kids who didn't have any because, 'You're a leader, Mr. Nightingale. *Lead.*'"

Marcus kept laughing even as he said, "Please don't worry about it. I'm not a friend type of person."

Lee wasn't laughing at all when he replied, "Yes you are."

Marcus's amusement ceased as well.

"If I remember correctly," Lee said, "you had Jet's back. And Roxie's. And Ava's. Wait, back up, you started with Indy's—"

Marcus interrupted. "Your point is taken."

"I'm not sure it is. It wasn't missed, Marcus. This isn't about you bein' one of those kids from Mrs. Zhang's class. This is about you already having a crew, but you leave us hanging."

Marcus said nothing because he didn't know what to say.

He didn't even know what he was feeling.

What he did know was what came out of his mouth. "You had Daisy's back."

"Damn straight," Lee returned. "And that shit's never happening again, but if she needs me, you need me, I'm there. Any of the men will be there. And that won't earn an invoice. Invoices don't happen when it's in the family."

Marcus turned his head and looked out the window.

Lee gave him a second.

And then he urged, "Come have a drink. My sister's getting married. I overheard just a hint of Indy's plans for her bachelorette. That shit hasn't even happened, and I already need fortification."

Marcus looked back at Lee.

And then he made a decision.

"Let's go."

Immediately, Lee smiled.

Marcus returned it.

Several hours later, Marcus walked into his and his wife's bedroom.

Daisy was on the bed with a plethora of magazines, her journal, a stack of self-help books (something she always bought but never cracked open) an open, partially-eaten box of Godiva, a glass of rosé on the nightstand, the bottle in a marble sleeve along with it, a pile of pillows stacked behind her and her phone to her ear.

She spied him, said quickly, "Gotta call you back, Shirleen, my man just got home."

She hit the screen, tossed the phone on the bed and stared at him.

He reached a hand to his tie, walking to the foot of the bed.

"I'm sorry, darling. I know I texted I'd be late, but just to fully explain. Lee and I got to talking. So we decided to stay for dinner."

She bounced up and magazines, books and chocolates went flying when she raced across the bed and threw her body into his arms.

As ever, he caught her.

She smiled down at him, "Has my man accepted his membership in the Hot Bunch?"

"Yes."

She threw her head back and cried, "Yippee-kay-yay!"

He smiled at her.

But when she looked back down at him, he kissed her.

Then he fell on her in the bed.

And sometime later, he helped her clean chocolate ganache out of her hair.

TRACK 10
ROCK CHICK REBORN

His Future

Moses

"Chill, baby," he murmured.

"Chill is not an option, my man," his woman replied.

At this comment, he heard nothing from the back.

This was both surprising and unsurprising.

At least with Julien, who had something to say or grunt at or at the very least verbally smirk about, with everything.

Moses was noticing, though, that since graduation a few weeks ago, and his official sign on with the Army, Julien was shirking off the last remnants of boyhood.

He was off to boot camp in a month. Maybe it was the fact he had weightier things on his mind. Maybe, in preparation for what he was about to face, he was fully letting the teachings of the men at Nightingale Investigations sink in.

Maybe he was just growing up.

Roman, on the other hand, finished growing up around a decade ago.

"They know how I feel about you," Moses reminded her. "And they're my girls. How is this going to go bad?"

He was at the wheel of Shirleen's Navigator (a rite of passage in their relationship, seeing as Roman nor Julien even blinked when she handed him, and not one of them, the keys).

He chanced a glance from the road to Shirleen and saw the look she was aiming at him.

He turned back to the road and chuckled.

"Nothing is funny, Moses," she warned.

"Be nervous, sweetheart," he invited. "You'll meet them soon, so you'll get over it soon."

They were joining his girls for dinner, meaning she and her boys were meeting his daughters for the first time.

The full Jackson onslaught, rather than them meeting just Shirleen first, had been Alice's idea.

"No reason to draw it out, Dad," she'd said like he had an IQ of forty. "You come as a package with us, right? So does she with her boys. Let's just get it all out of the way in one night. At Bastien's."

He couldn't fault her logic.

Though he had the sense that part of it was about her angling to go to Bastien's. It was her favorite restaurant.

Their turn with their mom was over that evening. Judith had her own car, so she was driving them to Bastien's. After dinner, he'd go home with his girls, Shirleen would go home with her boys, and he'd add more time spent in his head trying to figure out how long he had to wait to ask her to move in so, one day, he could just go home with her.

He heard Shirleen make a freaked noise, and he knew it was because Bastien's sign was in sight.

He decided to ignore that, and so did the boys.

But he felt his lips quirk.

He found a parking spot and they all got out.

But Moses halted in his intention to go to Shirleen and claim her.

This was because Roman had already done it, and Julien was standing sentry, eyes on Moses to share he needed to keep distant.

So they'd passed the rite of passage of Moses taking the wheel that night. And definitely in the last couple of months, the boys had given indication they were getting used to him and they liked him being with their mom.

But they were protective.

He loved that for her.

And they'd had her all to themselves for a while, and they were still adjusting to a new man in their midst.

He'd give them the time they needed.

Just as long as they didn't take too much.

Bottom line, he'd always have to share her with them, but she had so much love to give, that wouldn't be a problem.

Therefore, Moses hung removed while Roman, head bent to Shirleen and in her space, gave his mom a peptalk. She nodded. He spoke so low Moses couldn't hear him. She nodded again. Roman spoke more. She squared her shoulders and lifted her chin.

There it was.

She then turned to Moses. "Right, let's do this."

Moses smiled at her and finally made his approach. He took her hand and together they led the way inside.

He knew his girls were already there because he'd seen Judith's car outside.

And he was prepared for what was going to happen next because his girls were beautiful, and her boys were boys.

However, he wasn't prepared for *how* it happened.

Shirleen had told him both boys didn't discriminate, but for the most part, Roman liked white girls. Julien's attraction tended to lean toward Black.

So he figured it would be Julien whose interest would be piqued.

But when they'd walked up to the table Judith and Alice were already occupying, he noted that Julien had a wary, aloof smile on his face and was standing protectively close to Shirleen.

Roman, however, had his gaze locked on Alice, and he looked like he'd been struck by lightning.

Shirleen might have been nervous, but she didn't miss this.

Her eyes flew to Moses, and they got big.

This was the lot of any man with daughters. It wasn't as if it was the first time it happened.

However, it was the first time it happened when his Alice appeared to have been struck by that same lightning bolt. So far, with so much in the world she needed to fix, she hadn't really shown a lot of interest in boys.

That just ended.

Damn.

"Right, since everybody seems to be down with staring at each other, I'll do this," Julien stated. "I'm Julien. This is my brother Roman. And this is our mom, Shirleen."

He indicated his brother and mother with a jerk of his thumb.

Moses stepped up. "And these are my girls, Judith and Alice." He gestured both in turn.

"Hi," Judith said.

"Hey," Alice whispered, eyes still glued to Roman.

"Hey," he whispered back, his voice a low slither of velvet that held such invitation in that one syllable, even Moses felt drawn in.

Damn.

"Nice to meet you girls," Shirleen said warmly, and added hurriedly. "Let's all sit."

Roman, Julien and Moses bumped into each other, all intent to help Shirleen with her chair.

Judith laughed.

Alice sighed (still watching Roman).

Roman and Julien backed off and Moses moved in.

They had a round table so, at first, he was pleased Julien slid into the seat beside Alice.

Until Roman slid into the seat on the other side of Shirleen, which meant he had direct eye contact with his youngest, something he instigated immediately.

Moses shared some eye contact with Shirleen.

The expression on her face said both *It's not my fault!* and *It isn't like we didn't know this might happen!*

He hadn't been with her long, but he still could read that.

Judith waded in. "So, uh, you work for a private investigation firm?"

She asked this to Shirleen, therefore, she startled when she got three simultaneous answers of "Yes."

"You work for a private investigations firm?" Alice breathed toward Roman.

"Yeah," he answered.

"Wow, that's cool," she said.

"Yeah," he confirmed on a sly smile.

Moses turned his head again, leaned in and looked over Shirleen's shoulder as he whispered in her ear, "Kill me."

He heard her soft laughter.

Now it was him who didn't think anything was funny.

When he turned back, he saw Judith's attention on him. Him and Shirleen. But when he caught her gaze, she quickly looked away.

He didn't know how to read that, so, with no other choice at that moment, he let it be.

"It's the best outfit in the Rocky Mountain region," Julien bragged.

"I've heard of them," Judith put in. "There's books written about them, right?"

"Books you're not allowed to read," Moses warned.

"Whatever, Dad," she mumbled, aiming the side eye at her sister that was meant for him.

Two teenage girls, he knew what the side eye meant. Absolutely.

"What do you do there?" Alice asked Roman.

"I'm the office manager," Shirleen cut in swiftly so Roman couldn't continue to charm Moses's youngest with his ultra-cool badassness.

"I bet that's interesting," Judith said with a tentative smile at Shirleen.

"It sure is, pretty thing," Shirleen replied.

Judith's smile became less tentative, and it moved to her dad.

Right, okay.

That smile was all good.

The server came to take their drink orders.

"What's everyone getting to eat?" Moses asked when the server left.

The girls chimed in, Roman and Julien had never been there, so they took his cue to study their menus, as did Shirleen, even though he knew she'd already decided what she wanted. His woman was good at online research when it came to menus.

Things smoothed out from there, mostly because Julien demonstrated that he was, indeed, simply growing up. Or at least that was what Moses read in the *Jesus, man, cool it!* looks he was aiming Roman's way.

Reading these looks, Roman checked back in to what was happening and its importance, which was both good and bad.

Good, because Moses no longer had to bear witness to his daughter's yearning gazes at Shirleen's son.

Bad, because Roman was no longer returning those gazes, so Alice seemed confused he'd suddenly lost interest.

Which might be why, when their entrees were served, she tried to learn more about the boy who caught her eye.

"So, I don't want to be nosy, but we're all kinda in this together, and Dad told us you guys were adopted." She gave a sweet smile to Julien and added, "I mean, it's also kinda obvious, you know."

Julien smiled back. "Yeah."

"We were runaways," Roman announced, his attention fixed to Alice.

Her attention shifted right to him, then she sat completely still and stared at him.

Judith's gaze raced to her dad.

Shirleen's hand curled around Moses's thigh.

"I got shot," Roman continued.

Judith gasped.

Alice put her hand on the table like she needed to steady herself or she'd fall out of her chair.

Shirleen's nails dug into his thigh.

"When I got out of the hospital," Roman carried on, "Shirleen took me in. Sniff's more brother to me than most blood brothers are to each other, so where I go, he goes, and vice versa. That means he moved in too. We fell in love with her, she fell in love with us, we all decided to make our family official. We both turned eighteen, we made it official. That's how it happened."

At this point, Shirleen took away the one she had on Moses and put her other hand on Roman's forearm that was resting on the table.

"Who's Sniff?" Judith whispered across the table to her father.

He jerked his head to the side, Julien's way.

She nodded.

"Why'd you get shot?" Alice asked Roman quietly.

It was Julien who answered.

"We're tight with a lady who's a social worker at the shelter where we hung. Long story, but she had some bad guys after her, one who wanted to kill her. He got his opportunity, and Roam put himself in front of one of the bullets."

Alice lifted both hands to the base of her throat.

Now Judith was also staring at Roman.

Moses stifled a groan, because that kind of show of devotion would earn the same thing from his youngest for maybe the rest of time.

"He got me, but he still got her. Shot her twice. It's just that

Law's a survivor, so she survived," Roman muttered, a sliver of embarrassment now creeping into his words.

"Seems like you're a survivor too," Alice noted.

"Only because Law taught me how," he replied. He glanced at Shirleen. "And Shirleen did too."

"Law's the social worker?" Judith asked.

"Jules. Law's her street name," Julien answered. "I named myself after her because Shirl-Ike isn't a badass name, not to mention, it isn't even a name."

Judith laughed. Alice tore her eyes off Roman and laughed too.

After giving a visible squeeze, Shirleen took her hand from Roman's arm and carried on eating.

"And you're going into the Army?" Judith inquired of Julien, thankfully taking them out of a conversation that would only serve to make his youngest fall deeper for Roman.

"Ship out next month," Julien replied.

They managed more normal through the entrees and desserts, and through that, Moses was pleased to see the girls respond to Shirleen's unique blend of warmth and sass.

When they were finished, his family walked hers to their car and Shirleen handed out hugs to both his girls. He got handshakes from both her boys. And his girls looked happy their dad was happy when he kissed Shirleen on the mouth before he helped her in the passenger seat.

Roman was now behind the wheel.

He didn't pull from the curb, though, until Moses and his girls were in the car.

Shirleen raised good kids.

He'd paid for it, so even though it drove Judith nuts whenever someone else drove her baby, Moses took the wheel.

"So?" he asked, pulling out behind the Navigator after he adjusted the seat, something else that drove Judith nuts.

"I like her a lot!" Judith exclaimed, and she had to mean it, considering her dad just adjusted her seat. "Her Afro is *insane*. It's so cool. There's so much beauty in Black hair, and she's all about it."

He could not argue this because he felt the same way.

"Alice?" He directed this at the back seat.

"She loves them," Alice said.

"Of course she does," Moses replied. "They're her boys."

"No, I mean, Julien, he's obviously not hers, but if you were blind, you'd never know it. It's like they're *hers* hers. Not like she adopted them."

"It is like that," Moses concurred.

"I noticed that too," Judith said. "It was really sweet. I thought Julien was going to give us a talking to so we'd be nice to her when he first showed at the table."

"They're protective," Moses murmured.

"I like that for her. Sons should be protective of their mommas. Like daughters are protective of their daddies," Judith decreed.

"Exactly like that, sweetheart," Moses confirmed.

They let it lie then, and Moses didn't think it was a good idea to press further opinions out of them. It was one dinner. They all had a lot of getting to know each other to do. Shirleen was a beautiful, sharp, funny, kind-hearted woman with an enormous amount of love to give. His daughters were good girls to their souls.

They had time.

It was all going to be great.

That said, he was glad the first meeting was over. He loved his daughters, and Shirleen was the best woman he'd ever met, and although he didn't show it, he was nervous too.

He got them home and got them settled, not that there was much to that. They had the switching houses thing down, something that nagged his gut every time it happened. But it was part of their lives. Nothing he could do about it, and nothing he would, because the alternatives were either not have them or to have stayed with their mother, which was not going to happen.

He was in his bedroom, about to call Shirleen to get her take on the evening, when there was a knock on the door.

"Yeah?" he called.

Judith opened the door and peeked her head around. "Can we talk a second, Dad?"

"Always," he answered, throwing out an arm to invite her to sit with him on his bed.

As she came his way, he gave consideration to the consolidation of the households.

He liked his place in Stapleton. There was a ton of greenspace. It was small, a newish build, so upkeep was minimal. And he'd given Judith free hand in decorating it, so his girl was all over the place.

This included his bedroom, with the long, black headboard she'd selected that went well beyond the mattress on either side. There were also cubbies on either side for books and shit, free floating shelves in front of them for you to put other shit, and built-in gold lamps above the cubbies with swinging arms so you could aim them over your book, or out of the way.

She'd rested some cool African-inspired art on the ledge at the top along with some family photos.

And she'd found this dark-brown leather bolster she'd instructed him to rest his plethora of pillows against at the head when he made the bed. He hadn't been big on that bolster at the time of purchase, but now he couldn't deny, it looked good.

On the other hand, Shirleen had at least a thousand more square feet, and the place was stamped with her. Glamor and attitude and in-your-face-take-me-as-I-am style. He liked that style. He liked her. He liked being in her space.

It was going to be interesting to see what they decided.

"I gotta warn you about Mom," Judith announced when they were both sitting on the bed, Moses with one bent leg up on the mattress, turned to her to give her his full attention, Judith cross-legged, angled his way.

He expected her to dish on her newly love-struck sister, not warn him about their mother.

Shit.

"What's happening, sweetheart?" he asked, with practice, keeping his impatience for their mom out of his voice.

"Well, obviously, we had to dress nicer for Bastien's, which we did, and she noticed, and she asked why, and...I don't know. I don't know why I told her. It was my decision. I figure I told her because, first, she gets stupid when we keep things from her."

Judith, the eldest, noticed more of her mother's bullshit when it was happening.

Alice had baby birds that had fallen out of their nests to save, and bullies on the playground to tell off. She noticed it. But it took longer to dig under her skin than it did Judith.

"You shouldn't call your mom stupid, honey," Moses rebuked gently.

"She acts stupid sometimes, Dad. It should be called what it is."

She wasn't wrong. He didn't want his daughter to speak of her mother that way, but she wasn't eight anymore. She was nearly grown. Every day, she got closer to becoming the woman she was going to be. As much as he wanted to freeze them as his babies forever, he had to let her bloom into whoever that was.

On this thought, his phone rang. They both saw the screen said SHIRLEEN CALLING.

"Two seconds," he said to his girl, then took the call. "Baby, I'm talkin' with Judith. Call you back."

"Okay, darlin'. Since it's probably on your mind, just to say, all good here. But talk soon," she replied, and he heard the disconnect of her giving him what he needed before he did it himself.

Yeah, he had to figure out how to come home with Shirleen.

He put the phone down.

"I like her for you," Judith whispered.

He felt his chest get hot. "Sweetheart."

"I hate you alone when we're not here. You're too good of a guy to be alone."

Right, enough of this mature adult dad and maturing-to-an-adult daughter shit.

He pulled her out of crossed legs and shifted them into the bed, him against his big pillows and leather bolster, his girl tucked to his side with her head on his shoulder.

"Talk to me," he demanded.

"Okay, so I told Mom we were meeting you and your new girl-friend and her sons. It was after, when we talked about it in the car, that Alice agreed it was the right thing to do. I mean, obviously, since you wanted us to meet her, she's going to be around awhile."

"She is," he confirmed.

"So Mom's eventually gonna find out."

"She would."

"And I think she's mad about it."

He sighed.

She pushed up and looked down at him. "But again, Dad, *stupid*. She's married to another guy. Why can't she just *move on?*"

"I don't know, honey," he muttered, hating he didn't have the answers, and pissed at his ex because she was still finding opportuni-ties to put him in that place. He gave his girl a squeeze and shared, "I'm glad you and your sister are smart enough to read this for what it is. And I love how sweet and interested you were in Shirleen, Julien and Roman."

"Particularly Alice with Roman," she mumbled, settling back into her old man, sounding amused, and although this didn't amuse Moses, he liked to hear his girl was.

"Yeah," he grunted.

She giggled.

He gave her another squeeze. "And the bottom line is, there's nothing your mom can do about it."

"Doesn't mean she's not gonna dream up something to do."

"Maybe so, but it's not your problem. It's not mine. It's hers."

"She might try to make it your problem."

God, his baby girl.

"Listen to me, honey," he urged. "Don't take this on. Definitely not before anything happens. And not after. It's summer. You got that internship you're doin' and other than that, all you gotta concentrate on is havin' fun and bein' young. Next summer, you're gonna be graduating and getting ready for college, and then you're gonna be in college and then grown up and startin' your life. After that, you'll be *in* life and working for the money to pay your bills and findin' your way to get ahead. You warned me. I love you for it. But now, your job is done. Hear me?"

"I hear you, Dad."

"Wanna get your sister in here and watch a movie?"

She lifted up her head. "*Wakanda Forever?*"

"Haven't we already seen that?"

"If we don't pick one, Alice is gonna make us watch *Judas and the Black Messiah* again. It's a great movie, but we need a happy ending."

"*Boomerang?*" he suggested.

She shook her head.

"*House Party?*"

She rolled her eyes, then shook her head again.

"*Waiting to Exhale?*"

"God, Dad, get in the new millennium."

He grinned at her. "You pick. Go get your sister. And popcorn. I need to text Shirleen we're doin' movie night and I'll call her tomorrow."

She jumped over him and hopped off the bed.

At the door, she turned and warned, "You two can't gang up on me and make me watch *Poetic Justice* again."

"That movie is a classic."

"We've seen it seventeen times."

"Maybe...four," he contradicted.

"Whatever, we're watching *Girls Trip,*" she decided then flounced out the door.

Oh shit.

He hadn't seen that one.

He texted his woman that she had the stamp of approval, it was all good, they were doing a movie, and he'd call her tomorrow.

While he was looking up a rating and the trailer for *Girls Trip*, he got back, *Love that for you, baby. Like I said, all good here too. Talk tomorrow.*

So he was smiling when his girls, both of them this time, flounced back in.

Then he got another text with advice from Shirleen.

That movie...maybe fast forward through the grapefruit scene.

Oh *shit*.

He didn't expect it.

Even with the warning.

They'd had a good run. Nothing like this had happened in a long while.

Though, if it was going to happen, he would have thought at least it'd start with a shot across the bow.

Not a hammering on the door the first day the girls were back with their mother.

Or...not day.

Evening, seeing as he and Shirleen were in his kitchen making dinner together.

No one should bother you at dinnertime.

Not even your crazy ex-wife.

Shirleen looked to him, and considering she worked in a place where she knew the protocol for a lockdown when someone was armed and intent to breach the office (he knew all about it because he read it in those books, but she did confirm it), she was conditioned to reacting to a different kind of danger than he was about to face.

And that was her response to the hammering.

"Yvonne," he explained.

"Oowee," she mumbled, her beautiful, tawny eyes growing large.

He'd told her about Judith's warning. She hadn't said much, although her eyes had blazed with hellfire. She reined that in and just commiserated. This wasn't her way to share he was on his own, it was his cross to bear. It was her way to share she was as powerless to stop Yvonne as he was, so there wasn't much to say.

The hammering kept happening.

Those gorgeous eyes grew larger.

Moses got close and put his lips to hers. "I'll take care of it."

"You need backup, I know a man who has grenades," she offered, and close up, he could see the warmth in her eyes, the humor, but also the concern.

And it was then he knew he was in love with this woman.

He let that feeling settle in him, and somehow, the pounding at the door muted, everything around them grew hazy, and it was him and Shirleen in this world, and no other.

Moses snapped out of it when she tipped her head to the side and her gaze grew questioning.

"Keep Tex on standby," he joked, feeling her strength seep into him, and something more.

It wasn't that she was a survivor, but she was giving that to him too.

It was in her eyes. He realized it had been for a while.

She felt like he did.

Suddenly, he didn't give two shits Yvonne was at the door, except the part where he had to leave Shirleen to go deal with her.

"Gotcha," she replied, and that word was a little breathy.

But even so, with Shirleen, she might be joking as well, or she might call Tex when he went downstairs to the front door.

With regret, he left her and did that, opened it enough to stand in it, keeping his hand on the knob on the inside.

"I really thought we were done with this shit, Yvonne."

"It's my understanding you introduced our daughters to another woman."

"We've been divorced awhile," he reminded her.

"When things got serious with Demetri, I told you when they were going to meet him."

"You did. They were a lot younger then. And you didn't ask me if I was all right with it. You told me it was going to happen."

"And that makes a difference?"

"To me it does."

"Obviously."

Fuck, he was so damned tired of this shit.

"Yvonne, why am I standing here talking to you when I should be dealing with the chicken I got upstairs?"

"Because I'm not happy you didn't offer me the same courtesy as I did you."

He felt her, so he looked over his shoulder and up the stairs.

Shirleen was standing on the landing. Not curiosity. His woman had his back.

He lifted his chin to her.

She crossed her arms in front of her.

"Is she in there?" Yvonne's voice was pitched higher.

He returned his attention to her and forced her back by stepping out.

He closed the door behind him.

"Right, this conversation needs to be had," Moses began. "You could have called me with your concerns, but instead, you wanted to create a situation. To address this situation, yes. I'm seeing someone. Yes, it's serious. No, it isn't any of your business. No, you don't have any right to be pissed at me because I didn't warn you I was going to introduce her and her boys to our girls. You know me. I've dated. I've seen other women. I haven't introduced any of them to Judith and Alice because they weren't in my life in that way, so I didn't make them a part of my daughters' lives. I'm not that kind of man, I'm definitely not that kind of father. You know that too. So I don't owe you any explanations. And when it'll have no bearing on your life, I don't owe you any notice that I'm going to share something with our girls."

"I think we have differing opinions on that," she retorted.

"I don't give a fuck what you think."

Her head snapped back like she was avoiding a blow.

Moses kept at her.

"Since you're here, it gives me the opportunity to tell you, now that I've addressed this latest situation, I'm no longer going to get involved in any more. We share two beautiful, smart, sweet daughters. That's it. They're nearly all grown. There'll be some conversations we'll have to have, I'm sure. But other than those, you live your life, I live mine, and I'm done."

"You can't—"

"I can, Yvonne. Test me," he warned. "You stay here, pounding on my door, you won't be talking to me next. You'll be explaining to an officer of the law why you're pounding on my door after I told you I'm done talking and you need to go home. Now, I'll be sure to make that clear. I'm done talking. You need to go home. This continues, I'll get a restraining order."

She gasped.

"I'm not jokin'. Seriously. Test me. But just to say, this test, it's on you whether you pass or fail."

On that, he turned, walked in, closed the door and locked it.

He did the last part with eyes to Shirleen, who had jumped back when he opened the door.

"You couldn't stop yourself, could you?" he asked, feeling his lips twitch.

"I had to have my man's back."

"By eavesdropping?"

"Honey," she hooked arms with him, and they moved to the stairs, "that was hot." She mimicked his deep voice. "'On you whether you pass or fail.' Good parting shot."

His lips stopped twitching because he was chuckling. "I'm glad you approve."

"I'm thinkin' the chicken can wait. Shirleen needs some between-the-sheets time with her man to congratulate him for being calm and collected under duress, and still kicking ass, just verbally."

He was still chuckling as they made the living room, but he didn't guide them to the kitchen.

He guided them to the next flight of stairs, seeing as his bedroom was on the top level.

"You spoil a girl," she whispered, her eyes on him, and they'd fired.

"I wanna say this is all for you, and I'll be all about you, baby. But this is also for me."

"You bet your ass."

At that, he burst out laughing.

But she wasn't done.

"Though, you might need to give me five to call Tex and tell him so he can turn back with his grenades."

Moses's laughter got louder, even if he didn't know if she was joking.

And since he was all about Shirleen and how funny she was and what they were going to get up to next, he didn't even notice he'd closed the door on an ugly chapter in his past that had tried to haunt him.

And when he did, she didn't pound on the door, still trying to drag him back to his past while he guided his future to his bed.

Moses lay in bed and watched Shirleen, wearing his shirt, walk from the bathroom to the bed.

It was after chicken, greens, mashed potatoes and gravy.

It was after they watched a little TV.

It was after their second round of between-the-sheets time.

And seeing her in his shirt, those long, shapely legs on display, he was wishing he was twenty-three again so he could keep her up all night.

He threw back the covers.

She reversed her trajectory from her big tote, where she'd have a nightie, a clean pair of panties and her morning toiletries stashed, and she came to him.

She put a knee to the bed and joined him, getting close, tangling their legs, but sitting up on a forearm on the mattress at his side.

"Need to change, baby," she told him. "I fell asleep in your shirt once, remember? The buttons kept snagging the sheets."

"In a second, we need to talk."

Her expression changed from peaceful, post-chill night spent together, post-coital to alert.

"You okay?"

"I met the boys. We instigated sleepovers, here, not at yours, in deference to your sons. You and the boys met my girls. You eaves-dropped on a situation with Yvonne."

She smiled.

He felt his lips twitch again but kept talking.

"Today, before you got here, I cleared out two drawers and some closet space for you."

Her brows shot up.

"No more nighties in your purse," he declared. "Bring some over to leave. And double up on toiletries."

"Ooo, my man. Doubling up on toiletries. I can't wait to tell the Rock Chicks. They'll throw a party."

He laughed.

"No, really," she asserted. "They'll throw a party. Cashews and everything." She snuggled closer. "But I'll make sure someone makes pigs in a blanket."

He kept laughing, regardless that he knew she didn't lie. She'd been holding back the RCs from throwing a Shirleen's Got a Man party since they got together, so she was now holding them back by a thread.

He got serious, wrapped an arm around her and pulled her closer.

"It's time for the next step, baby."

"I'm in."

He let out a slow breath, happy that was where she was at, happy that she so easily gave it to him.

"So then, next up, and I'm not talking now. We're not ready. The kids aren't ready. But when we're ready, we need to have discussed it so we know what we're gonna do."

"You mean, who's going to give up their kickass crib to move in the other one."

He fucking *loved* they were on the same page.

"That's what I mean," he confirmed.

"Okay, I gotta say, Moses, my house is the only safe home my boys have ever had. I know Judith pimped this place out for you, and it's gorgeous. So maybe, if we pick my place, we can give her a budget and she can redo my livin' room." She thought about it. "And maybe my dining room."

He also loved that she offered that.

Even so.

"You have a big house, Shirleen. You and me, when all the kids are going to be gone soon, we don't need that much space. Julien is going to be in the Army, and he's probably not ever going to move back in." He watched the cloud pass through her eyes at the thought of her son leaving her, so he didn't delay moving on to the next. "And Roman will probably stick around for a while, but not long."

She nodded. "He's already savin' for a down payment on a car and a deposit for an apartment. He's in training with Lee, but even in training, Lee pays well. He might need a roommate for a year or two, but he's already warned me, he's wanting his freedom."

"Okay, so..."

He let that hang.

She picked it up. "So, Christmas. Thanksgiving. Their birthdays. My birthday. Fourth of July. Eventual wives and babies. When they went fifteen years with no safe space they could call their home, I want them to have the next fifteen years knowing it's there, waiting for them, on holidays and whatever might come."

"You're right," he muttered.

"I'm sorry," she whispered.

"Why?" he asked.

"You obviously have reservations."

"No, except your boys will be gone, but I'm sensing you'll want to keep their rooms as they are, and we have three more years of high school with Alice, one with Judith, and summers when they come home from college."

"I hear you," she replied. "And they each have their own rooms here. But at my place, Judith could take the guest room upstairs. We can convert the junk room downstairs for Alice."

"Isn't Roman's room downstairs?"

Her lips curved up. "Okay, maybe Judith downstairs and Alice upstairs."

"How about we talk to them?" he suggested. "This isn't happening tomorrow. You put your stuff in your new drawers, double up on toiletries, we can wait until Judith graduates, and maybe they'll be down with bunking together during holidays and summers when she's home from college."

"My man with a plan."

He grinned.

She leaned in and kissed it.

When she pulled back, she cupped his face with her hand and stroked his cheek with her thumb.

"You sure you're okay after Yvonne came callin'?"

"Old Yvonne would have pounded on the door again after I closed it in her face. Maybe she heard me this time."

"Maybe." She didn't sound sure.

"It doesn't matter."

"It does if it upsets you," Shirleen disagreed. "It does if it upsets Judith."

"Judith gets upset because I get upset. If I don't get upset, which," he gave her a squeeze, "baby, I got no reason to be upset. Then like I said. It doesn't matter."

He wrapped his other arm around her and pulled her full on his body.

"She's the past," he whispered. "I got my future in my arms and that's my sole focus. Yeah?"

"Yeah," she whispered in return.

"Love you, Shirleen Jackson."

He'd never said the words.

That was why her tawny eyes fired and stayed warm as she melted into him.

"Love you too, Moses Richardson."

He slid a hand to the base of her neck and pulled her to him.

And Moses embraced his future.

His future embraced him back.

The End
Thank you for revisiting the Rock Chick Universe!

Join the next Rock Chick Generation
on romantic adventures as they
expand the Nightingale Investigations team.

Avenging Angel
the story of Raye and Cap.

READ MORE FROM KRISTEN ASHLEY

Avenging Angel

Rachel Armstrong has a burning need to right the world's wrongs. Thus, she becomes the Avenging Angel.

And maybe she's a bit too cocky about it.

While riding a hunch about the identity of a kidnapper, she runs into Julien "Cap" Jackson, who was trained by the team at Nightingale Investigations in Denver. Now he's a full-fledged member at their newly opened Phoenix branch.

It takes Cap a beat to realize Raye's the woman for him. It takes Raye a little longer (but just a little) to figure out how she feels about Cap.

As Raye introduces Cap to her crazy posse of found family and his new home in the Valley of the Sun, Cap struggles with his protective streak. Because Raye has no intention to stop doing what she can to save the world.

But there's a mysterious entity out there who has discovered what Raye is up to, and they've become very interested.

Not to mention, women are going missing in Phoenix, and it seems like the police aren't taking it seriously.

Raye believes someone should.

So she recruits her best friend Luna, and between making coffees, mixing cocktails, planning parties and enduring family interventions (along with reunions), the Avenging Angels unite to ride to the rescue.

AVENGING ANGEL
AVENGING ANGELS BOOK ONE

To all the Rock Chicks out there.

They're all for you,
but this one in particular
is my love letter to our history...
and our future.

Chapter One
Natural Badassery

"I'm gonna go in."

"Are you *insane?* You can't go in!"

"I'm just gonna have a look around."

"What if you're right? What if this guy is the actual guy?"

"Then I'll call the police."

"What if he sees you?"

I sighed. "Luna, this isn't my first rodeo."

"Exactly!" she cried in a Eureka! tone. "So, yeah, let's talk about that, Raye."

Sitting in my car, talking to my bestie on the phone and casing the house in question, I cut her off quickly before she could start in— *again*—about how she felt about what I'd been up to lately.

"I'm just going to wander across the front of his house and look in the windows. No biggie."

Truthfully, I was hoping to do more than that, but my best friend of all time, Luna, didn't need to know that.

We'd had chats about what she called my unhinged shenanigans, or my lunatic tomfooleries. Then there were also my deranged mischiefs (Luna read a lot and her vocabulary showed it).

But I did what I did because, well...

I had to.

Luna spoke into my thoughts. "Okay, so if *I* kidnapped a little girl from my church, and *I* was holding her for things I won't even contemplate why someone would do that, and some woman I'd never seen in my neighborhood casually strolled in front of my house and looked in my windows, what do you think *I* would do?"

"Sic Jacques on them, whereupon he'd lick them and dance around them and race away, only to race back, bringing his toys so they'd play?"

Jacques was Luna's French bulldog. He was gray, had a little white patch on his chest, and I considered myself for sainthood that I hadn't dognapped him yet. I was pretty sure I loved him more than Luna did, and the Tiffany's dog collar I'd splurged and bought him (which she refused to let him wear because she said it was too bougie, like that was a bad thing) proved my case on that.

"This isn't funny, Raye," Luna said softly.

That got to me, her talking softly.

She was yin to my yang, Ethel to my Lucy, Shirley to my Laverne, Louise to my Thelma. Dorothy to my Rose/Sophia/Blanche (and yes, I could be all three, dingy, sarcastic and slutty, sometimes all at the same time, I considered it my superpower).

You get the picture.

We were opposites, but she loved me.

And I loved her.

"I promise to be careful. It's gone okay so far, hasn't it?" I asked.

"Luck has a way of running out."

Hmm.

I struggled for a moment with the use of the word "luck," considering I thought I was pretty kickass, but I let it go.

There was a little girl missing. And I had a feeling I knew where she was.

"I need to do this, Luna."

It was her turn to sigh, long and loud.

She knew I did.

"Call me the instant you get back to your car," she ordered.

"Roger wilco," I replied.

"You don't even know what that means," she muttered.

"It means I heard you."

"Yes, it also means *you will comply with my orders*. That's what wilco is short for."

See?

She totally read a lot.

"Okay, so, samesies, yeah? I heard you, and I'll call."

Another sigh before she said, "You won't call because either, a, you'll be tied up in some villain's basement, and I'll then be forced to put up fliers and hold candlelight vigils and harass the police to follow leads. This will end with me being interviewed, weeping copiously, naturally, saying you lit up a room in a Netflix docuseries about solved cold case files once some hikers find what's left of your body at the bottom of a ravine in fifteen years. Or, b, you won't get anything from the guy, so you'll start devising some other way of figuring out if it's him or not. You'll then immediately begin scheming to implement plans to do that, at the same time you'll remember you forgot to buy tampons for your upcoming cycle, and you need to pop into CVS, after which you'll realize you're hungry and you'll stop by Lenny's for a cowboy burger and a malt."

She was hitting close to home with that first bit, and she knew it.

Including when my period was coming, something she always reminded me to prepare for because I always forgot, and as such, was constantly bumming tampons from her. Though, her remembering this wasn't a feat, since we were together so often, including working together, we were moon sisters.

"I will totally call," I promised.

"If you don't, I'm uninviting you to my birthday party."

I gasped.

"You wouldn't," I whispered in horror.

Yes, you guessed it. Luna threw great parties, especially when she was celebrating herself.

"Try me."

"I'll call. I'll absolutely call. Long distance pinkie swear."

"Lord save me," she mumbled, then stated, "If you hit Lenny's, *definitely* call me. Since I brought Lenny's up, I now realize I need a malt."

After that, she hung up on me.

I leaned forward and put my phone in the back pocket of my pants, my eyes on the house that was just right of the T at the end of the street where I was parked.

There was a light on to the right side of the front door.

He was home.

He was home, and he might be the kind of guy who grabbed little girls to do things it wasn't mentally healthy to contemplate.

Maybe Luna was right. Maybe this was madness.

Though...

Her name was Elsie Fay. She was six years old. She had a cute-as-a-button face.

And she'd been missing for nine days.

What could happen, even if he saw me?

He wasn't going to storm out of his house and confront a stranger who was out for an evening stroll.

I was just getting the lay of the land.

I was correct in what I said to Luna.

No biggie.

That said, better safe than sorry.

I leaned across to the glove compartment, opened it and nabbed my stun gun. I then got out, locked the doors on my bright yellow, Nissan Juke (not exactly a covert car, I needed to consider that on upcoming operations) and shoved the stun gun in my free back pocket.

I'd dressed the part. Navy-blue chinos and a navy-blue polo shirt with a yellow badge insignia at my left breast.

Sure, under the yellow badge it said PUPPY PATROL, and this was my uniform when I did moonlighting gigs for an online dog walk-ing/pet sitting service. But if you didn't look too closely, it appeared official. If someone asked, I could say I worked for code enforcement or animal control or...something.

I'd seen in an episode of *Burn Notice* that the best way to do something you weren't supposed to be doing, somewhere you weren't supposed to be doing it, was to look like you were supposed to be there doing what you were doing.

And if a burned TV spy couldn't guide me in a possibly, but not probably, dangerous mission, who could?

Okay, so I was seeing some of Luna's concern.

Nevertheless, I walked up the sidewalk toward the house in ques-tion like I'd personally designed the neighborhood. I hooked a right at the T, walked down the street a ways, crossed, then walked back up on the possible perp's side of the street.

And then across the front of his house.

Good news, his window shades were open.

More good news: I was right, he was there. And as I'd already ascertained, and this cemented it, he was sitting, watching TV, and he looked the nondescript everyman version of your not-so-friendly local kidnapper. The image of a man whose neighbors would appear on TV and say, "He gave us a bad vibe, but he was quiet and didn't cause any trouble, so..."

I kept walking, thinking she could be in there.

In that house.

Right now.

Scared and alone and so much more that, for my mental health, I refused to contemplate.

Not many homes in Phoenix had basements, and his place was a one-story ranch. I couldn't imagine he'd be stupid enough to keep the shades open in a room he was keeping a kidnapped little girl in, but who knew? Maybe he was.

I couldn't call the cops and say, "Hey, listen, hear me out about this guy."

I had to have something meaty.

At the end of the street, I turned right, then hooked another right to walk down the alley. It was dark, impossible to see the words Puppy Patrol on my shirt. I was counting the houses in my head at the same time coming up with a plausible explanation of why I was wandering down the alley should someone stop and ask.

I hit his back gate without seeing anyone and tried the latch.

Of course, locked.

If I owned a home, I might lock my back gate to deter intruders. But it'd be a pain in the ass when I took out my garbage.

If I was holding a little girl I'd snatched, I'd definitely lock it.

Hmm.

The dumpsters and huge recycling bins were just outside his gate.

Perfect.

This meant I could get into his yard to look in the back windows, though I might not be able to get out.

I'd figure that out later.

I climbed on top of the dumpster (not easy and all kinds of gross), stood and looked over the top of his fence.

Clean landing on turf.

He should xeriscape. We were in a water crisis. No one should have lawns anymore in arid climates.

Right, I totally needed to learn better focus.

I looked at the house.

Light on in the kitchen with no one in it (did this man *not* hear about climate change?). No lights on in the other side of the house. I couldn't tell from that far away, but it seemed like no blinds were closed over the back windows, because I could see the light shining in from opened doorways to a hall.

Except the last room, but it might just be the door was closed.

This could mean he had nothing to hide.

It could also mean he was an idiot.

Well, I was currently harboring fifty thousand forms of bacteria on my hands and clothing from my climb onto the dumpster. In for a penny, in for a pound.

I put one foot to the top of his fence then leaped over. I landed on soft knees and it still jarred me like a bitch.

Ouch.

Right away, I set the pain aside and returned my attention to the house.

No movement in the windows. I didn't think I was making that much noise, but, if he could hear it, I hoped my climb onto the dumpster sounded like someone taking out their trash like people often did at seven at night.

Though it appeared I was good.

Sticking to the fence, I moved left, forward, then crouching, I went in.

Coming up from the crouch just enough to see over the windowsill, I noted it was a window to the dining room, through which was a galley kitchen, through which was the living room and him sitting in a recliner watching the Diamondbacks on TV.

Okay, good. He hadn't heard me and come to investigate.

Onward.

Crouch-walking under the window, I hit a back patio. The first window there, from the dim light shining in from the rest of the house, I saw was a bathroom.

The next room, door open from the hallway, more light shining in, appeared to be an office.

The next room, there were blinds, they were down and closed.

"Shit," I whispered.

I went around the side of the house, which was rife with mature trees, not a lot of room to move. I shimmied my way in, but the blinds on the window on that side were also closed.

Open windows everywhere else, except this room.

That was fishy.

Right?

Still not enough to call the cops.

I couldn't now say, "I have a feeling about this guy, and the blinds on one of his rooms are closed, though I can't tell you how I know that. So obviously, that's cause to break down the door and search the house ASAFP."

They weren't going to rush an urgent call to assemble the SWAT team on that intel.

Time for tampons, Lenny's and scheming some plan to find a way to get into that house and check that room.

I was thinking a trip to a T-shirt printer and some time on my computer creating a bogus notice from the city for a mandatory visit from pest control.

Gophers.

I'd heard gophers were a sitch in the Valley.

Though, not so much inside houses.

Again, I'd figure it out.

I was about to move out of the trees, hoping the lock on the gate was easy to navigate from the inside, when I noticed movement at the window.

I froze.

I'd brushed against the trees, but I didn't think I'd made much noise. Surely not enough he'd hear me three rooms away over the TV.

That was when she appeared.

Just her head.

Dark hair: messy.

Cute-as-a-button face: terrified.

Lips: moving with words anyone could read, even in the dark.

Help me.

Adrenaline surged throughout my body, making it tingle top to toe.

Tears flooded my eyes, making them sting.

My heart clutched and memories battered my brain, trying to force their way in.

I couldn't give them free reign or they'd paralyze me.

It took mad effort, but I held them back using the aforementioned adrenaline and the sight of her face in that window.

I was right.

She was there.

I had to call the cops.

Now.

I put my hand to the window, nodded to her, tried to smile reassuringly, my mind cluttered.

Should I call from where I was? Would he hear me? If he did, what would he do with her? He had access to her. I did not. He had access to his garage. I did not. And I was at least a five-minute run away from my car, and in my current situation, couldn't even easily get around to the front of the house to see which direction he'd have gone. Had a neighbor heard me, one who would maybe warn him someone was lurking on his property, or they'd called the cops and their sirens would do it? Would me being in his backyard, trespassing, mess up the investigation?

I had to get to the alley and make the call.

Pronto.

It's going to be okay, I mouthed back to her. *Someone will be here soon.*

Panic filled her little face. Even if I suspected she couldn't read my lips, my guess was she knew I had to leave. She shook her head.

I pressed my hand into the window, not that she could notice the added pressure, so I got closer and mouthed, *Promise. Hang tight.*

She kept shaking her head, but I was on the move.

I didn't stick to the fence. I ran right to the back gate.

The latch locked from the inside, but with an easy twist and lift, the door opened.

On instinct, I looked back to the house and froze yet again.

I saw a shadow moving through the hall across the door of the bathroom, headed toward the back bedroom.

"*Shit!*" I hissed.

I sprinted back to the dining room window and didn't bother crouching.

I looked right in.

I was correct about that shadow.

He wasn't in his recliner anymore.

He was headed to her.

"No, no, no, no, no," I chanted, panic creeping in, attempting to take a firm grip.

To force it out (because that would paralyze me too, and no way could I let that happen), acting fast, even though I was not able to think as fast, I had to go with it.

I went to the patio door and knocked, loud.

And I kept doing it until he showed at the door.

Okay, good.

Or, also, bad.

What the heck did I do now?

The door was made of glass.

Through it, he looked at me.

He looked at the patio beyond me.

He looked at me again.

And I looked at him.

On the wrong side of middle age, my guess, closer to sixty than forty. His shoulders were broad. His hair was thin. He had a little gut. He needed a shave. And he had to be four or five inches taller than me.

I had a stun gun and thirty years less than him.

But he could probably take me.

Expressions chased themselves across his face. Shady. Incredulous. And regrettably, he ended on angry.

He opened the door and demanded, "Who are you and what are you doing on my back patio?"

"Hi!" I exclaimed. "I'm so sorry." I pointed to the badge on my chest. "I work for Puppy Patrol?" I told him in a question, like he could confirm I did. I didn't wait for his confirmation, I babbled on. "And I was walking one of your neighbor's dogs. He slipped the leash and ran off. I'm trying to find him. He's a little Chihuahua. I'm freaked! He'd be a snack for coyotes."

"We don't have coyotes in the city," he informed me.

"Yes, we do," I contradicted. And we did. I had a Puppy Patrol client (actually, it was a Kitty Krew client, same company, brown uniform, whole different ball of wax) who'd learned that the hard way. "They come down from the mountains and in from the desert, easy pickin's for people who let their cats go outside and stuff."

RIP Gaia.

"How did you get in my backyard?"

"Your gate was unlatched," I lied. "And I could swear I saw little Bruiser dash in here from the alley."

He leaned out to look toward his gate.

I leaned back, my hand moving toward my pocket and my stun gun.

When he looked back at me, I knew he saw through my story.

And it was on.

I didn't have time for the stun gun. Not now.

He lunged.

I tried to evade.

He caught me anyway and pulled me right inside.

Totally knew he could take me.

Damn it!

We grappled.

I went for the gonads with my knee and hit his inner thigh.

This caused him not to let me go, but instead grab my hair and pull, *hard*.

Jerk!

I went for the instep, slamming down on it with my foot, and that was better. He yelped, his hold loosened, I ripped myself away from him (pulling my own hair, because his grip hadn't loosened that much, *ouch!*), and I yanked out the stun gun.

He recovered too quickly, nabbed me, and even if I knew he could take me, I was still surprised at his strength when he wrenched me around at the same time throwing me down to the floor with such force, I hit the tile and skidded several feet. My head then struck a corner of his kitchen cabinet.

Worse than the hair pulling. Seriously.

While I blinked the stars out of my eyes, he came after me, reached down to grab me again, and I remembered I had my stun gun in my hand.

I turned it on, heard it crackling, his attention went to it, and ill-advisedly in our current positioning, I touched it to him.

He went inert, then dropped, all two hundred some-odd pounds of him landing square on top of me.

"*Oof*," I grunted.

Fuck! I thought.

I dropped the stun gun to try to shift him off, when my breath that had just come back stopped because he was suddenly flying through the air.

He landed on his back several feet away from me, his head cracking against the tile with a sickening sound.

But I didn't have any attention to give him.

I didn't because there were two men standing over me, and these two dudes could totally take me. I didn't know who they were. They might be associates of the bad guy. But they were so gorgeous, for a split second, all I could think was that I'd be okay with that (the them taking me part, that was).

One was tall, very tall, with black hair, green eyes and an age range of thirty-five to a very fit, healthy-living, great-genes forty-five. He also looked familiar, but I couldn't place it in my current predicament. And last, he'd had some goodness injected in him from, my guess, a Pacific Islander parent.

The other one was also tall, very tall, just not as tall as the other guy. I'd put him in the thirty to thirty-five age zone. He had dark-brown hair, full, short, but the top and sides were longish and slicked back in a stylish way. He had a thick brown beard that was trimmed gloriously and gray-blue eyes.

For a second, I thought he was Chris Evans.

Then he spoke.

Angrily.

"What the fuck are you doing?"

Wait.

What *was* I doing?

Oh yeah.

Suddenly confronting a Chris Evans doppelgänger, I'd forgotten about Elsie Fay (that sounded really bad, but trust me, with these guys, who wouldn't?).

I shot to my feet and dashed through the kitchen.

That was as far as I got before I was whipped around with a strong hand on my arm and Chris Evans was in my face.

"Again, what the fuck are you doing?" he asked.

"Who are you?" I asked back.

"I asked first," he returned.

"Do you know that guy?"

"What guy?"

"The one who owns this house."

"No."

Okay, I was going with he was a good guy. Maybe a cop. Maybe they were onto this guy like I was.

Yeah.

Anyway, if they were in cahoots with the bad guy, they wouldn't have cracked his head on the tile.

So I was going with that because there was no more time to waste.

"Elsie Fay," I said, tore my arm from his hold and raced through the house.

I made it to the door to the room at the end of the hall and was in such a rush, when I turned the knob, I slammed full-body into it because it was locked.

I then grabbed the knob and jostled it and the door violently, like that would magically open it.

I was pushed aside with an order of, "Stand back."

I did as told.

"Are you a good guy or a bad guy?" I belatedly asked in order to confirm.

"Even if I was a bad guy," he said while positioning in front of the door, his eyes aimed at it, "I'd tell you I was a good guy."

Excellent point.

He lifted a beefy (those thighs!), chocolate-brown-cargo-pants-clad leg and landed his boot solidly by the door handle.

The door popped open.

I slipped in front of him to enter the dark room.

I immediately tripped over something, but stopped, righted myself and called into the darkness, "Elsie Fay?"

No movement. No sound.

Chris Evans entered behind me, *close* behind me. So close, I could feel his heat and the natural badassery that wafted off him (this apparently happened with guys who knew how to bust open doors with their boot), and I felt him move.

On instinct again, I spun and whispered, "Don't turn on the light."

The other guy was standing in the doorway.

I turned back to the room, and gingerly, my eyes adjusting to the dark with weak light coming in from down the hall (trying to ignore the fact this room would be pitch black without the door open, and how that would affect the mind of a little girl), I called, "Elsie Fay? It's me. From outside? You know, the window? You're okay. We're gonna get you out and call the cops and your parents and—"

I didn't finish because a six-year-old hit me like a bullet. She slammed into my legs so hard, I nearly went down. And I would have if I didn't run into Chris Evans and his hands didn't span my hips to hold me steady (told you he was close).

I didn't have time to consider how those hands felt on my hips.

Elsie Fay was clawing up my chinos.

I bent and pulled her into my arms. She was heavy, as six-year-olds were wont to be, too big to be held, too young to realize it, though in this instance, she needed it, and I didn't have time to consider her weight as she clamped onto me with arms and legs. She, too, fisted her hand in my hair and she did it tighter than the bad guy. She also shoved her face in my neck.

"It's okay," I whispered to her. "You're okay. You're safe now. Okay?"

She said nothing.

I turned to Chris Evans and his hottie partner.

"Is he neutralized?" I asked.

"Yes," the hottie partner answered.

"Then let's get her out of here," I stated, and didn't wait for their response.

I pushed through them and got that little girl the hell out of there.

Avenging Angel is available to purchase in all formats

NEWSLETTER

Would you like advanced notification about Upcoming Releases?
Access to exclusive content? Access to exclusive giveaways? The first
to see a new cover reveal? Sign up for my newsletter to keep up-to-
date with the latest from Kristen Ashley!

Sign up at <u>kristenashley.net</u>

ABOUT THE AUTHOR

Kristen Ashley is the *New York Times* bestselling author of over eighty romance novels including the *Rock Chick, Colorado Mountain, Dream Man, Chaos, Unfinished Heroes, The 'Burg, Magdalene, Fantasyland, The Three, Ghost and Reincarnation, The Rising, Dream Team, Moonlight and Motor Oil, River Rain, Wild West MC, Misted Pines* and *Honey* series along with several standalone novels. She's a hybrid author, publishing titles both independently and traditionally, her books have been translated in fourteen languages and she's sold over five million books.

Kristen's novel, *Law Man*, won the *RT Book Reviews* Reviewer's Choice Award for best Romantic Suspense, her independently published title *Hold On* was nominated for *RT Book Reviews* best Independent Contemporary Romance and her traditionally published title *Breathe* was nominated for best Contemporary Romance. Kristen's titles *Motorcycle Man, The Will*, and *Ride Steady* (which won the Reader's Choice award from *Romance Reviews*) all made the final rounds for Goodreads Choice Awards in the Romance category.

Kristen, born in Gary and raised in Brownsburg, Indiana, is a fourth-generation graduate of Purdue University. Since, she's lived in Denver, the West Country of England, and she now resides in Phoenix. She worked as a charity executive for eighteen years prior to beginning her independent publishing career. She now writes full-time.

Although romance is her genre, the prevailing themes running through all of Kristen's novels are friendship, family and a strong sisterhood. To this end, and as a way to thank her readers for their support, Kristen has created the Rock Chick Nation, a series of programs that are designed to give back to her readers and promote a strong female community.

The mission of the Rock Chick Nation is to live your best life, be true to your true self, recognize your beauty, and take your sister's back whether they're at your side as friends and family or if they're thousands of miles away and you don't know who they are.

The programs of the RC Nation include Rock Chick Rendezvous, weekends Kristen organizes full of parties and get-togethers to bring the sisterhood together, Rock Chick Recharges, evenings Kristen arranges for women who have been nominated to receive a special night, and Rock Chick Rewards, an ongoing program that raises funds for nonprofit women's organizations Kristen's readers nominate. Kristen's Rock Chick Rewards have donated hundreds of thousands of dollars to charity and this number continues to rise.

You can read more about Kristen, her titles and the Rock Chick Nation at KristenAshley.net.

facebook.com/kristenashleybooks

instagram.com/kristenashleybooks

pinterest.com/KristenAshleyBooks

goodreads.com/kristenashleybooks

bookbub.com/authors/kristen-ashley

tiktok.com/@kristenashleybooks

ALSO BY KRISTEN ASHLEY

Fire Inside

Ride Steady

Walk Through Fire

A Christmas to Remember

Rough Ride

Wild Like the Wind

Free

Wild Fire

Wild Wind

The Colorado Mountain Series:

The Gamble

Sweet Dreams

Lady Luck

Breathe

Jagged

Kaleidoscope

Bounty

Dream Man Series:

Mystery Man

Wild Man

Law Man

Motorcycle Man

Quiet Man

Dream Team Series:

Dream Maker

Dream Chaser

Dream Bites Cookbook

Dream Spinner

Dream Keeper

The Fantasyland Series:

Wildest Dreams

The Golden Dynasty

Fantastical

Broken Dove

Midnight Soul

Gossamer in the Darkness

Ghosts and Reincarnation Series:

Sommersgate House

Lacybourne Manor

Penmort Castle

Fairytale Come Alive

Lucky Stars

The Honey Series:

The Deep End

The Farthest Edge

The Greatest Risk

The Magdalene Series:

The Will

Soaring

The Time in Between

Mathilda, SuperWitch:

Mathilda's Book of Shadows

Mathilda The Rise of the Dark Lord

Misted Pines Series

The Girl in the Mist

The Girl in the Woods

The Woman by the Lake

Moonlight and Motor Oil Series:

The Hookup

The Slow Burn

The Rising Series:

The Beginning of Everything

The Plan Commences

The Dawn of the End

The Rising

The River Rain Series:

After the Climb

After the Climb Special Edition

Chasing Serenity

Taking the Leap

Making the Match

Fighting the Pull

Sharing the Miracle

Embracing the Change

The Three Series:

Until the Sun Falls from the Sky

With Everything I Am

Wild and Free

The Unfinished Hero Series:

Knight

Creed

Raid

Deacon

Sebring

Wild West MC Series:

Still Standing

Smoke and Steel

Other Titles by Kristen Ashley:

Heaven and Hell

Play It Safe

Three Wishes

Complicated

Loose Ends

Fast Lane

Perfect Together

Too Good To Be True